THE REMAINS

First published by Charco Press 2023

Charco Press Ltd., Office 59, 44-46 Morningside Road, Edinburgh
EH10 4BF

A CIP catalogue record for this book is available from the British Library.

ISBN: 9781913867478
e-book: 9781913867485

www.charcopress.com

Edited by Fionn Petch
Cover designed by Pablo Font
Typeset by Laura Jones
Proofread by Fiona Mackintosh

Margo Glantz

THE REMAINS

Translated by
Ellen Jones

CHARCO PRESS

For Ariel
And for the mourners

Dying, we head towards our death…

Pedro Calderón de la Barca

As I spoke to you, my dear, this afternoon,
and your face, expression, actions made it clear
that all my words were leaving you unmoved
I wished that you could see my heart laid bare.
Then Love, seeing my attempts, came to my aid,
although it seemed impossible a task,
and in the form of tears spilled out in pain
she helped me to distil my broken heart.
Enough, my dear, enough, relent, let lie;
let jealousy's cruel tyranny now cease,
may vile suspicions and imagined signs
cast no more stubborn shadows on your peace.
For now you've seen and in your hands you've held
my broken heart, in liquid humour, here distilled.

Sor Juana Inés de la Cruz

Castration has a second function: it permits the disruption of the voice's natural pitch. It liberates the human voice from its dependence on sex and age.

Pascal Quignard

If I can take a breather, the pain has stopped.

Mono Blanco

Lastima, bandoneón, mi corazón,
tu ronca maldición maleva…
Tú lágrima de ron me lleva
hasta el hondo bajo fondo
donde el barro se subleva.
Ya sé, no me digás, tenés razón,
La vida es una herida absurda,
y es todo, todo tan fugaz,
que es una curda, nada más,
mi confesión…

La última curda
Cátulo Castillo and
Aníbal Troilo

My heart, bandoneon, is hurt
by your filthy words, loutish, slurred.
Your tears of rum drag me to hell,
deep underground, where the clay rebels.
I know, don't tell me, you're right!
Life is an absurd wound,
and it's all, all so fleeting
that to confess this is to drink
myself to death tonight…

One Final Binge

My name is Nora García.

It's been years since I last came to the village: I park my car, then go shyly, warily, up to the front door and into the house. I barely recognise it, it's changed, and not for the better, the garden's overgrown, the plants are dry, the grass is yellowing, there are patches of bare earth where before there were flowering shrubs. Down in the ravine – flame trees, trees with wide canopies. The place is full and I almost lose my nerve, my heart shrinking: there are a few people I know, no one I'm especially fond of, and perhaps others I've forgotten: it's been a long time. There's a woman I think I recognise, though her body looks bloated, her face too, and she looks a bit off-colour – a funereal colour, perhaps? I'm exaggerating, I tell myself, it's the news of his death, coming back to this house, the fear of remembering too much, the inevitability of seeing people I hate, people who have hurt me – the usual, I tell myself, uncertainties of the heart. The woman's name escapes me. She's looking at me – mockingly? derisively? or is she just saying hello? Perhaps that's just how people look at you at funerals, perhaps that's just life, to use an old phrase of my mother's, rest her soul – as Juan is resting now, or at least I hope he is, I really do hope he rests in peace.

I nod to the staff looking after the house, then head to the living room where the body is laid out. It's a large room (enormous, really), full of musical instruments and sheet music scattered over a long table beside the computers and blank manuscript paper (sheet music, do people still use sheet music?).

I look around, scanning the wall-to-wall bookshelves packed with books – that's how it should be, books go in bookshelves, or ought to – the paintings on the walls alongside patches of damp.

Several people standing around the coffin.

I go over.

Like all coffins, this one has a kind of window – or is it a door? – so you can see part of the body. His face is pale, I suppose that's as it should be, it's simple, really, he's dead now and dead people's faces have no colour in them, his heart has stopped beating, that's all, I tell myself, that's all there is to it, he's dead now. He's dead, he's no longer breathing, his heart has stopped beating, his blood has stopped flowing. I start peering around nosily, then stop and ask myself how I'm feeling, but the truth is I don't feel anything, anything at all, my pulse beats calmly, regularly, normally, a hundred beats a minute. There's a strong smell of mildew invading everything, the room, the coffin, my body, I smell of mildew now, of damp, intense damp. Someone moves away from the coffin and I approach in order to see better, see him better, to see Juan better. I lean over, my cheek almost touching his face – his hands are folded over his chest and he's holding a cross: I didn't expect that. His face is such a strange colour, olive, sallow! As if he were dead, I think, that must be it, that's what's happened, yes of course, it's so simple, he's dead: his heart has stopped beating. A small, greying, or rather ash-coloured moustache covers his lips, thinner now than ever. His skin is transparent, his cheekbones protruding, his high, boxy forehead framing sunken eyes, the eyelids tight shut. The white pine wood coffin with gold inlay; several wreaths leaning against the walls, obscuring the paintings. Wreaths on the bookshelves too, obscuring the books. Candles, next to the coffin – four of them. And a cloying smell, the smell of mildew (why am I surprised by this? it's always hot and humid here), the thick smell of mildew. Juan is wearing a light, straw-coloured jacket that matches his pale face and the colour of the wood. His tie and shirt are the same hue. It's an improvised chapel, full of people, paintings, books, musical instruments, a long grand piano, propped open – a Bösendorfer, with sheet music sitting on the rack; next to it is the harpsichord with its open top, exquisitely decorated in a baroque design, a softly-sketched, pastel-coloured, almost idyllic landscape (where's the Steinway? I can't see it). Over in the corner, a woman dressed in black, a crestfallen figure. Next to me, a clean-shaven man wearing coarse cloth trousers and a straw hat as though to protect him from the sun in this sunless room. A dog comes in, skeletal, skin clinging to her bones, yellow teeth, pointy snout, dark teats sagging – she's recently given birth and looks to be starving. Nobody shoos her out of the room – she comes over to the coffin, grazes me with her tail, peers around nosily (just like me), then lies down so that her black teats – so many of them! – spill onto the floor. I lean over the coffin again to see him better, to observe him, to grasp every detail of his death (the death of his body), and what I find is a strange cross in his hands and a wispy, lead-grey moustache – is it hard? stiff? waxed? – a moustache that completely transforms his appearance, disguising it, degrading it.

A woman offers me a drink and I accept, pulling myself together (it's a tequila, an Herradura Reposado) (a short, very well-dressed, polite-looking man comes in, approaches the coffin, and asks the woman serving the tequilas, in a voice – a diction – that carries further than his stature might suggest: is it you, madam, to whom I

3

ought to offer my condolences? Shaking her head, the woman hurries to the front door.) (Shouldn't he have asked me? Shouldn't he offer his condolences to me?) (To me, Nora García?). I can't rid myself, will never manage to rid myself of this cloying smell of mildew or clotted blood. It's turning my stomach. I leave the room, bumping into someone who says hello, but I don't reply, I head for the courtyard, trying not to look at anybody: the smell is surrounding me, dogging my every step, heavy. It's hot, very hot, and I'm poorly dressed in a jumper, trousers and boots. I recently had my hair cut, thankfully, and it makes me look younger. I pretend not to know the people who gave me so much grief while I was with Juan, when the children were still children and the dogs and cat used to play together – contrary to all expectations, they never fought like cats and dogs, but played; they may as well have been the same species, breed, sex, the female dog sometimes mounting the male, the male sometimes mounting the female, all of them jumping, panting, flinging themselves at each other, the cats and the dogs, or just the dogs, though I should say the cat (singular) and the dogs, because there was only one cat and lots of dogs, all of them piling on top of one another, playing in innocent frenzy (the garden is very large) (there are a lot of plants, a lot of trees at the back of the property), the dogs would growl, howl, bark, lick, bite or bare their teeth at each other, wind their tails together, white or golden or chocolate or black, long-haired or short-haired, the acrid smell of cat invading everything, of a tomcat pursuing a mate.

In the courtyard, tall men, short men, some very elegant, others in informal or very simple clothes, one man with a shaved head entirely covered in tattoos, fat women, like the one I've already described, who I look for but is nowhere to be found; instead, a young woman with a dark fuzz over her upper lip; so many mourners – are they grieving? – with lacklustre or ruined complexions, dark-skinned, olive-skinned, tanned, pale, blue-eyed, black-eyed, brown-haired, all kinds of moustaches, others clean-shaven, some dressed plainly, others too elegant for a house in the countryside, but all of them, without exception, including the man with the tattoos (how strange! didn't it hurt when he got all those drawings done on his forehead, all over his skull and the back of his neck?) with a glass in hand, talking, laughing, gesturing. One group, in particular, of men in well-cut cashmere suits, stands looking uncomfortable: there's a stiffness that's in keeping with their moustaches, which almost all of them have, though in different shapes and sizes (only one of them has a beard); yes, I can't help but notice the abundance of moustaches, bristling, stiff, luxuriant, unkempt or well-smoothed, small, long, curly, blonde, brown. One man has a black moustache that hides a shy little smile. Another one, blond this time, has a stubbly, unkempt looking chin and a very long blond moustache, so long it curves right up, almost to his eyes, and he is twisting one of the tips between the fingers of his right hand. The tall, handsome man, with (light) brown skin, has a thick, dark, silky, well-cut moustache, and is smiling broadly, like a rabbit. Juan, too, has grown a stiff, uneven moustache. I watch them all out of the corner of my eye – there's a solemn, put-upon look about them, and even though they've had plenty to drink their bodies are as stiff as musical instruments – like cellos, for instance – and whenever anybody goes over to say hello, the ritual, affectionate backslapping reverberates, counterpointing the mariachi band's tuneless trumpets, guitars, and violins, the mariachi band's endless singing (their faces sallow, their flesh worn) (their moustaches trembling as they sing) in their dun-coloured charro suits, their fake silver

5

buttons, their faded ties in the colours of the national flag, the two lines of buttons down the seam of their trousers accentuating their knock-kneed stance. In another group there are two women dressed similarly, as though one is a replica of the other, one blonde, the other dark, one tall, the other small and slight, one with serene blue eyes, the other with a reddish flash in her gaze, dressed almost identically; one is in a long skirt suit and high-heeled sandals and the other in a trouser suit and moccasins, but both their outfits are white, as though they're on holiday at some luxury beach resort. White suits at a funeral, I ask myself. Why not? One of the women is wearing a lot of silver necklaces, the other, smaller one, diamond rings and gold necklaces: a catwalk, a magazine piece featuring socialites. A man directly opposite me, lost in thought, puts one hand on his crotch. He's tall, dark-skinned, with light hair and green eyes, and he opens his mouth to reveal two gold eye teeth. Next to him, the mariachis are still singing – the mariachis sang – and the buttons on their suits are made of cheap, tarnished metal. One of the mourners, dressed very formally, approaches them and starts singing (loudly, passionately) a song by José Alfredo Jiménez as though it's an aria: the abrupt twang of a broken string; he plants his (small) feet wide so as to sing better, and his moustache quivers. Nearby are several campesinos with palm leaf sombreros and sallow faces, haggard flesh, in white shirts and jeans or in the old Indigenous style, in rough cotton trousers. A dwarf – is he a flautist? Waiters with trays of canapés and glasses of tequila continue to do their rounds (why is there no wine? isn't red wine supposed to turn into blood?) and in the kitchen the staff are preparing food – the thick stink of reheated oil is infecting the air.

The guests are mostly made up of professional music-ians – pianists, singers, sopranos, contraltos, basses, baritones, countertenors, conductors, cellists (I'm a cellist), violinists and violists, oboe players, saxophone players, composers, scholars and academics, a male flautist (who plays the transverse flute), a female flautist (who plays the recorder), a drummer, and a critic who writes for culture supplements. What did I expect? Could it have been any other way? There's nothing strange about seeing a famous flautist, percussionist, or opera singer in the house of a recently deceased composer, conductor, and exceptional pianist – is there?

Have more tears been shed over funerals than over death itself?

This big living room – where the body is laid out – really is full of instruments, isn't it? Dozens of them, along with old sheet music, CDs, books about music, biographies of composers. Sheet music? Yes, sheet music, too. CDs and sheet music – Bach, Schubert, Pergolesi, Haydn, Monteverdi, Handel, Schumann, Beethoven, Vivaldi, Campra; whole CDs of piano music, just of soloists: Glenn Gould, Horowitz, Rubinstein, Wilhelm Kempff, Walter Gieseking, Benedetti Michelangeli, Sviatoslav Richter, Claudio Arrau, Marta Argerich, András Schiff, Emil Gilels, Vladímir Ashkenazy, María Joaõ Pires, Radu Lupu. There's vinyl too, and an old record player; a lot of CDs and DVDs showing memorable performances of nineteenth-century and baroque operas, with Callas, René Jacobs, Kathleen Battle, Teresa Stratas, Andreas Scholl, Cecilia Bartoli, Pavarotti, and Plácido Domingo singing; a CD of the last castrati with their mewling voices, where they sound like cats being castrated. I remember those records, I can practically hear them (the old ones, on old, heavy, 78 rpm discs: Caruso, Tebaldo, Vickers, Chaliapin, Schwarzkopf), I can practically hear the players, practically see them, forever singing their arias, gesticulating, mouths wide and arms raised high, majestic, declamatory, in Aida and La Traviata, in Orpheus (and Eurydice), Dido and Aeneas, Ulysses (the return of) and Xerxes (by Handel) (very fashionable these days), sung by David Daniels, a countertenor (in French they say haut-contre, in Spanish, contratenor).

I go back into the house, into the living room where the body is laid out: the air is humid and sticky. There are two half-empty glasses on top of the piano, one of them with a dark lipstick stain on it. I find a space for myself next to the coffin and lean over, staring at Juan, observing him morbidly, scouring the details of his face, his attire, the coffin. I list them, voicing some of my impressions out loud, very quietly, as though praying, I murmur them, accompanying those who are praying the rosary, as though my murmuring might help blot out the heavy smell of damp. How strange, I say to myself again, they've given him a cross to hold on his chest! God, his hands were so beautiful! His chest, that shield of bone and muscle protecting the heart! (The heart is only a muscle, a pump that irrigates the body, an extraordinary machine) (I smell of cigarettes). His face is a sepulchral colour. What colour did I expect it to be? I'm intrigued by his moustache, so faint, so grey, wispy – ash-coloured, really – uneven – has it been waxed? He never used to have a moustache, he looks like a caricature, a parody; a moustache that's not quite salt and pepper but rather the colour of burnt straw (like those enormous, wonky haystacks in the fields on the drive to the village, like his corduroy jacket), the coffin in pale, unfinished wood with all that gold inlay, the wreaths propped up against the walls exhaling their heavy smell. Still, neither the scent of the flowers nor of burned wax mitigates the cloying smell surrounding the body like a halo, spreading, enveloping me, it's beginning to choke me, I can't bear it. I lean over his face again, watching him, looking at him, looking at his face, his body – well, what I can see of his body – going over the details again one by one: the nondescript necktie he's wearing, the greenish, straw-coloured jacket, the rough-hewn, white pine wood coffin, the ordinariness of it. Juan, yes, Juan, who so loved tailored clothing, his fine (designer) ties, impeccable shirts (made to measure, always tasteful), cashmere jumpers, Armani suits, Balenciaga ties. That's a shame, I can't see his shoes – I wonder what colour they are? And his socks? (Am I losing it?) I look up at his face again. How could I not have noticed before? A black handkerchief is holding up his jaw, exaggerating his pallor, contrasting with the burnt straw of his suit, it goes with the colour of the wood but not the cloying smell of clotted blood that's surrounding me, circling me like a halo.

I close my eyes, I can see him now, stretched out in front of me, practically naked on a table, his body full of needles – in his chest, his stomach, his ears, above his eyebrows, in his world-weary forehead, even in the skin of his neck, a taut needle beside the jugular. I don't sleep out of tiredness any more, and every time I dream about him, it's a different life I've lived. I'm still standing by the body, his eyes closed, a needle near the smooth skin of his belly button. A faint red mark traces the needle's journey; black silky hairs on his stomach and chest, his delicate rosy areolae, his almost non-existent nipples. Every time I dream about him, my eyes always closed, it's a different life I'm living, the needles piercing the middle of the forehead, his forehead, mine, death's, death coming to close his eyes, my eyes, eyes that died when they saw him, when they saw him like that with two needles at an angle, trembling as though in anticipation, vibrating on the bone. I reach out my hands, put the right one on his left leg, which trembles, he lifts it, bends it, I run my hand slowly over it then touch his knee, I lean over him and

9

place my palm on his warm chest, life is an absurd wound, it pierces my heart, his heart is calm (fifty to a hundred beats per minute), the blanket covering him slips open to allow me a glimpse of his left thigh and I tremble, I tremble like I did when we were young, a hundred beats a minute – more? palpitations? The heartbeat – my heartbeat – increases, that's for sure: the heart is only a muscle, a pump that irrigates the body, keeping it alive (the heart sends venous blood to the lungs for oxygenation, then retrieves it as arterial blood and immediately distributes it around the entire organism). My heart: I wore it on my eyes, as the poem goes.

I open them and there he is again, motionless, the idea of death by needles enthrals me, the viewing window in the coffin leaves his face visible, his pallor, that ill-judged, greying moustache, stiff and useless, the black handkerchief confining his jaw, the moss green jacket, the nondescript tie (underneath his clothes, his heart has stopped beating), and that smell, always that smell, the thick, suffocating smell of mildew.

I can't settle anywhere – I go outside again, moving jerkily, heading for the garden. There are scattered groups near the borders, on the uneven ground down towards the ravine. People are treading on the lawn, dropping stubbed-out cigarettes (or lit ones) on the rosebushes. Nearby, bougainvillea climbs the walls, its colour as bright as the trumpets' metallic blasts. Snatches of conversations can be heard (I dreamed I was lost), loose words (I woke up furious), spilling out (I didn't know who I was), hypocritical sentences: they're heavy, some of them strike a chord (to whom should our deepest condolences be offered? somebody asks, a rhetorical flourish worthy of a great leader), they form a mutilated language that still etches itself onto the skin like a tattoo. Tattoos: they cover his flesh, the air, masking the pain, the pain of needles piercing the skin, shield, mask, Medusa. Only that which does not exist is real. The heart has impulses that reason does not know. A callous person, unmoved by others' pain, has a heart of stone. Ezekiel says so in the Old Testament: God does spiritual transplants of hardened hearts. The patient who received an artificial heart just died of a heart attack – his metal heart failed.

I can see and hear a man in the garden, surrounded by people, talking loudly and inanely: It might seem hard, but it's deceptively easy, he says. I'm serious, dying is simple, you die when your heart stops – you failed, heart – that's all, it's simple. Eduardo is an old friend of Juan's (and of mine, too, at one time) who gives me an imperceptible wink of recognition, and repeats: It's deceptively simple, his heart just burst. He is huge, bearded, and old. In one of his hands – immense, furrowed, fleshy, hairy, vast – he is holding a glass of tequila (King Kong carrying the blonde damsel in distress as he climbs the Empire State Building) and his droopy eyelids give him a sleepy look, despite the fact his eyes are enormous and wide open. His nose is thick, his mouth thin but important, his lips pulled taut, the corners turning up to meet his saggy eyes: he does not have a moustache. When he speaks, his lips pull back into a greedy, disdainful grimace. A pale woman, small and svelte, well-dressed with neat hair, wearing no makeup nor a single piece of jewellery – austere-looking (reptilian?) – (her heart tainted by the sickness of the world?) smiles mechanically, standing next to Eduardo, making him resemble a giant. The rest of them look on, enthralled: several different ideas are tangled together in the banality of what he's saying. A voice comes from behind him, a leathery-looking man with a sweet, shy moustache: It's not like death goes around whispering in our ear, though, does it? It just arrives, suddenly, when we least expect it. Silence falls and I move away – he's right,

11

I think, death doesn't whisper in our ear, it just arrives, alone, without warning us in advance. I don't care how simple dying or anything else is for that matter, even if it was that simplicity that made his heart explode, made it shatter into pieces (mine too), yes, life, the absurd wound that is life, yes, it's true, the heart is only a muscle that irrigates the body, keeping it alive, a muscle that one day fails us.

I wander from the garden to the courtyard, from the courtyard to the (very large) garden. I settle near a railing. Down in the ravine: tall trees with large canopies, a few flame trees in blossom, their branches stretching, dislocating, a red flower on each tip. I can't bear the noise, the imagined signs, the clinking of glasses, the smell of mildew, the stubborn shadows, the words brought to me or whisked away on the wind, the vile suspicion that takes me by surprise, the malice, the hypocritical sentences. I take out a cigarette and am about to light it (smokers are twice as likely to suffer from a cardiac arrest). Is that you, Nora? I recognise the voice, gentle and deep and sombre, and look up to see a woman standing there. Yes, I'm Nora, I reply. It's been so long, she says, I'm glad I found you because I didn't have anyone to offer my condolences to, and her voice changes register: darker. She is a blonde woman, tall, slightly stooped, I can't quite recall her name. I'm María, she adds. I arrange my face into a routine expression that could mean several things – that I remember her, that I don't remember her, that I'm happy to see her again, that I'm indifferent. Did you visit him? she asks. I went to the hospital, to the high dependency unit. He was all nervous, he'd lost so much weight that his false teeth didn't fit any more. He didn't enjoy having me there, on the contrary, he was furious I'd seen him like that, wrecked, unrecognisable. Of course, she says, because he was so, so handsome. He didn't like people seeing him in that state, she repeats; and the truth is she doesn't want to listen to me, she's not interested in what I have to say, she wants to be the one talking, she wants to tell me her own version of Juan's illness (and his death). She explains that when he could no longer breathe properly – how odd is this? she says – he started growing a moustache. She tells me about how he struggled to breathe, how he felt asphyxiated, about his pacemaker (an Argentine named Favaloro was one of the inventors of the pacemaker), about the oxygen tank he had to carry around with him everywhere, about the blood clot in his lung, how they had to puncture the pleura to extract the fluid, about the intense pain this had caused him, about him almost suffocating to death that night and many others, about the everyday violence that comprises the life of a sick person: exhaustion, depression, the drip, the needles, the drugs, the doctors, the pacemaker, the defibrillator (in case of real emergency), the angioplasty, the bypass between the aorta and the coronary arteries. Her tale doesn't affect me much – rather, I'm fascinated by the way she tells it (hear me with your eyes), the way she moves her mouth so quickly, I can't understand what she's saying any more, I don't care, I've zoned out, hypnotised, watching how she spits her words frenetically, her lower lip starting to thin as she talks; her upper lip, much thicker than the bottom one, gradually disappears too, and by the time she says: it breaks my heart just thinking about it, her lips pressed bitterly together, by that time she no longer has a mouth, she has swallowed it, her face has split in two, a bloody wound slicing across it, the edges of which are clearly visible, an intense red (crimson?) (the absurd wound that is life), leaving a dark trace. The smell of mildew that's following me and that previously surrounded the coffin like a halo now settles in that scar; it's a faint smell, almost imperceptible at first, but becoming more and more noticeable, hot, cloying. The smell and the wound are clotting, forming a gummy mass made of expressions, gestures, and the incessant, indefatigable repetition of the word heart. I feel sick, my pulse starts to slow (less than a hundred beats per minute now), the voice gets louder, words spin round me as I slip and lose my footing and the smell is dragged down with me, sinking with me, deep underground, where the clay rebels. María interrupts her speech, and when she pauses her mouth is recovered entirely (the upper lip fuller than the lower one) (the bright red toned down), she places a hand on my shoulder, holding me up, looking at me worriedly. With an immense effort I grab hold of the railing, come back to myself, gasping a little, calming myself down, and without missing a beat María picks up from where she left off and begins to lose her mouth again in the process. I'm feeling better and set about listening carefully to her, but as before the asymmetrical shape of her mouth distracts me, the (full) upper lip and the long, thin, lower one, pressed bitterly or fearfully together, destined to disappear: life is an absurd, red wound. I can still see the outline of the mouth in a single colour, a darker lip pencil – a fragment of lip peeps out, disappears, then appears again. I concentrate, fascinated, on the movement and the colour – what colour is it exactly? cherry? crimson? It's a funereal colour, that's all I know – cyanosis? I stare at her, hypnotised, hearing without understanding the incessant noise coming from her mouth, words uttered quickly, unevenly, distortedly; through her teeth (their whiteness contrasting with the bright red of her mouth), like a basso continuo (on the cello or the harpsichord), you can hear, above all else, the word heart.

She stops abruptly, her nasal, metallic voice falling silent. She starts to say goodbye, leaning over to kiss me on the cheek, patting me affectionately on the shoulder, and, holding out her hand (I say this from the heart, she assures me), she quickly mumbles her condolences. I respond mechanically, and something I say – I'm not sure what – stops her short, or rather captivates her. She looks at me, makes a gesture and, like she's been wound up, immediately takes up her tale once more, her lips start to blur, her bottom lip shrinks and fades, the shape of her face changes; her fuller upper lip takes a bit longer to lose its consistency but eventually her face splits in two, she swallows her teeth (she looks like Juan when I visited him in hospital), eats her own mouth, make-up and all, the live image of a heart wounded by misfortune, of lips pressed bitterly, impatiently together.

Why do you ask that? Didn't I just tell you? Didn't I explain that he couldn't breathe? Didn't you know he was that ill? Honestly, just thinking about it breaks my heart (the coronarography (literally, an X-ray of the coronary arteries) allows them to visualise the arteries feeding into the heart by injecting an opaque contrast product, which can sometimes cause an allergic reaction). They did an angioplasty on him. Do you know how it's done? A probe with a little balloon is inserted into the femoral artery through a small incision in the groin, widening the arteries and dissolving the clot (which can be fatal). They then insert a stent to prevent a new (and always probable) obstruction. I can hardly describe what it feels like, telling you this, my heart aches (Juan's heart had stiff, thick walls, much thicker than normal, his blood didn't flow evenly, his lungs didn't oxygenate it very well, that's why they filled up with liquid and had to be punctured – very painful), you know what it's like, you know him, I mean, you knew him, you knew him really well, you knew what he was like, didn't you? You must remember. He was proud, very proud, he never complained, he never talked about his illness, not once did he mention his operations or that he had artificial arteries, he was in the hospital for ages, did you know that? Medicine's getting more and more sophisticated, doctors have new technologies all the time to help prevent or cure heart disease, but it was too late, his heart was already too far gone, too deteriorated, the heart, you know, is only a muscle that irrigates the body. When we saw him again, after the operation, he looked so different, can you imagine? He had this wispy, uneven moustache, he couldn't go anywhere without an oxygen tank, yes, did I tell you he couldn't breathe? (apparently, all his teeth were false). You might think you've got a heart of steel, but no, I promise you, any one of us could suffer from heart failure.

Yes, I reply, yes, you're right, his heart failed – you failed, heart – his broken heart in his hands (in the doctor's hands) (in the operating room), that heart which previously shattered in my hands – life, I say to myself, life, that useless, absurd (red) wound. (I read a remarkable story in the newspaper: a French doctor called Marescaux operated remotely, from New York, on a patient in Strasbourg. He directs a robot's movements according to what he sees on a screen (the robot's three articulated arms hold the surgical instruments and a camera) in order to carry out a gallbladder ablation. The patient on the hospital bed is covered from head to toe with a sheet (only a very small part of his reddish stomach can be seen). Next to him, watching motionlessly, like the figures in that famous Rembrandt painting, are three doctors, or anaesthetists, masked and dressed in pale green scrubs, ready to intervene should it become necessary.) (Open-heart surgery has also been performed remotely.) (Artificial heart transplants have been performed: the patients died, or almost all of them did: yesterday I read that one managed to survive and return to his hometown, an ordinary town in the US Midwest where he was given a hero's welcome. The man (in the photo in the New York Times) is looking out the window of an enormous truck driven by one of his sons-in-law, where he sees a wall of people applauding and the local band playing a triumphant march. The man (he's about sixty – how many years has he got left?) smiles broadly, his teeth perfect.)

Very quietly I say, María, look how many people have come to his funeral, you really think nobody knew he was sick? How did they find out he'd died? And there was me thinking he'd die alone like a dog. It's no use, she's not listening to me, she never listens, she doesn't want a conversation, she likes talking, leaping from one phrase to the next, once she's on a roll nothing can stop her, she's focused on that word-producing mechanism that immediately eliminates her mouth from her face: He was in hospital for days, I didn't tell anybody, it felt awful, nobody knew he was ill, so ill his heart was barely working. When they discharged him he started using the oxygen tank, and don't you think it's strange he kept the moustache? what did he do that for? what was he hiding behind that stiff little moustache, indelible as a tattoo? Incredible, really, he kept travelling, honestly, can you imagine? (concert tours?) (how did he play the piano while he was hooked up to an oxygen tank?) I smile and she interrupts herself: what's funny? No, nothing, I say, pushing a lock of hair out of my face, the hair I had cut before coming to the funeral, that haircut that makes me look younger – thank goodness, it makes me look younger – no, I reply, I was just remembering something, but her attention lasts only a second, she is distracted and now I make no effort whatsoever to understand what she's saying, stubborn shadows, imagined signs. I distract myself by observing her attire, she's dressed in the latest fashion, with a sombre touch very appropriate for a funeral – discreet earrings, light make-up – she has class! A good haircut, I think, like mine, it makes her look younger too. I admire her impeccably cut silk blouse – Armani? (a designer I adore but whose clothes I never buy because I'm cheap). Why did I come so poorly dressed to this funeral? A pearl grey pashmina is wrapped around her neck (it might even be a shahtoosh – it's delicate, with flowers in different shades of grey embroidered round the edges (darker than the rest of the cloth, and in the middle there's a red, maybe cherry-coloured circle – the colour of the flowers on the tips of the flame tree's naked branches?), yes, pastel-coloured pashminas are very fashionable these days, although the truly elegant prefer to buy a delicately soft shahtoosh, they're warmer than sables and weigh nothing at all!) (why wear a pashmina somewhere this hot?). Her shoes have a low heel, very simple – perfectly elegant – her trouser suit is a deep crimson, almost black, perfectly cut (of course) (Emmanuelle Khanh, a label hardly anyone knows around here). She's still talking, hurriedly, as though her very life were at stake, as though she were performing Marin Marais's variations, the ones the French composer wrote for the viola da gamba – an instrument used in the seventeenth century as a continuo, a constant, stubborn accompaniment – and which I can hear right now, adapted for the recorder, yes, Marais's Follies of Portugal, whose frenetic, convulsive rhythm is eased by the slender but intense – persistent – sound of the transverse flute. That's how María talks, sometimes her voice is sharp, sometimes deep, she's very good at modulating her tone to enliven her tale, and – didn't I say? – her voice reminds me of the English countertenor, David Daniels, whose register is metallic and nasal. I interrupt her from time to time, monotonously, with my refrain: Yes that's true, you're right: it is what it is, as my mother used to say, that's life, the open wound that is life. Then very quietly, I add: And there was me thinking he was going to die alone like a dog (and, as we all know very well, dead dogs don't bite)!

I murmur to myself, skipping from one idea to another, some of María's words triggering old memories. That time, for instance – Juan and I still lived together – when I was sitting in a corner reading a Dostoyevsky novel (which I often ritually re-read), many years ago, many shocks, inertias, journeys, deceptions, many love affairs ago. In the memory I'm always sitting down (today, I'm sitting in a chair someone has abandoned, near the coffin. María has followed me into the living room, pulled over another chair, and settled down in front of me to repeat her story, insatiable) (varying it, perhaps like the variations Beethoven composed on an air by Diabelli or Paisiello, or like Johann Sebastian Bach's Goldberg Variations). Yes, sometimes we're sitting in our other house, which is very cold, especially in winter, Juan and I sitting and talking with a group of friends, and, yes, drinking a glass of something. On other occasions we're sitting in a restaurant chatting with some friends and one day, it might have been in December, an overbearing woman we know who is gesticulating like a lager lout buys a round of tequilas to celebrate something or other, and even though no one wants to let her pay she pulls out her cash like a character from The Idiot (is it Rogozhin who tosses his roubles into the fireplace to impress Nastasya Filippovna?) and we all look at each other in consternation, helpless in the face of her power play, and in the middle of the memory (as though to give the lie to it) María's words reach me, one by one: …he was days and days in hospital and didn't tell anyone, nobody knew he was sick, we thought he'd gone travelling like he always used to (carrying an oxygen tank around with him?), we thought he'd gone travelling, travelling (on a concert tour? how did he manage to play the piano while he was hooked up to an oxygen tank?) (high blood pressure, alcohol abuse and tobacco, sometimes a sedentary lifestyle, sometimes frequent travel, the hospital, the angioplasty, the hospital, the open-heart surgery, the pacemaker – Favaloro, the Argentine, shot himself in the heart). Her tedious chatter is making me drift off. I still can't make head nor tail of my memories, the only thing that's clear is that I'm always sitting down in them, sometimes in front of a typewriter or computer, wanting to tell a love story, or playing the cello, or reciting sad poetry by someone like that Chilean poet, or copying out tango lyrics and desperately wanting to cry (while eating chocolates filled with cherry liqueur), but I restrain myself, life is an absurd wound, it's all so fleeting, I don't want to humiliate myself by crying in front of María! Will she notice my eyes have gone red? I needn't worry, she's so absorbed in her story she can't hear a thing, she can only hear herself (hear me with your eyes!), she utters incoherent words that reach me in snatches, interrupting my memories, and I focus only on her mouth, that scar splitting her face in two. She lets out a deep sigh, shadows surround us like a halo, stubborn shadows, imagined signs, and the intense (cloying) smell of mildew.

Can she smell it? Or is it just me?

And I write, I'm still writing, sitting in front of my machine. Juan and I used to live together; I used to help him correct his writing or his scores, before we had computers, when we still had to use a different sheet of manuscript paper for each instrument, sheet music, yes, that relic from another time: now everything is written directly onto a computer and copyists have gone extinct,

Mozart writing the last notes of his Requiem by candle-light, he'd be obsolete, or Rousseau renouncing the world to spend his mornings copying sheet music to earn a living, absurd (neither absurd nor obsolete, simply a non-existent occupation, a trade that's been quite forgotten). Many things, I say to myself, are obsolete. I smile – how banal! The banality of attending a funeral, of being among all these – what are they, mourners? Of being just another guest, am I just another ordinary guest?

I'm sitting in this big living room, silent and cold, listening to Mozart's Piano Concerto No. 20, Köchel something-or-other has just finished but the CD player's still going – it can hold up to five CDs – and my friend, the other one, the one from my memory, the woman from the restaurant, the one who's like Rogozhin (well, no, because Rogozhin is small, sickly, and insignificant. Does that matter?) repeats her imperious but magnanimous gesture in this restaurant where we are seeing in the new year – are we seeing in the new year? which year? – this is my night, she says, and insists on paying the bill even though it means burning through her entire bonus (austerity measures) and we accept, resignedly, and drink and drink until we can no longer see straight. I am still at the typewriter or computer or in the restaurant with that overbearing friend or by the coffin listening to María (who right now is recalling the uniqueness of her position): she talks and talks, with less and less mouth, that horizontal scar, the absurd wound that is life, its fleetingness, that stubborn, endless babbling that undermines her handsome attire. I am still sitting at the typewriter, inert, copying the complicated score for Juan's latest composition by hand (that's how Anna Magdalena Bach used to do it, the composer's second wife, and many of his manuscripts still have her notes on them, including the definitive version of the six

Solo Cello Suites. Rousseau, too, copied music to earn a living, paid per sheet, after he decided to become a recluse). Again, a character from Dostoyevsky comes to mind, one who Juan often recalls – we're both sitting by the fireplace in our house, having returned from the restaurant after that friend of ours bought everyone dinner en masse and against their will, and she too is sitting next to me, or opposite the fireplace, unlit despite the fact it's winter and the house is freezing, her unwelcome Rogozhin-esque mannerisms recall the unforgettable scene in which, to prove his love for Nastasya Filippovna, Rogozhin arrogantly tosses a bundle of roubles into the fire, the lit fireplace in a nineteenth-century Russian living room (but no, let me correct the memory, it's not Rogozhin, it's Nastasya Filippovna who throws a wad of a hundred thousand roubles into the fireplace, wrapped in newspaper).

My shoes are made of black satin, with an ankle strap and a stiletto heel, my tights are sheer black with a (very straight) seam, my black dress is made of silk georgette with rhinestone appliqué (I look like I'm off to dance a tango) (I'm a cellist and Juan is a pianist as well as a composer), our overbearing friend, on the other hand, is wearing flats and a thick, navy blue, V-necked jumper to hide her broad shoulders, she's dark-skinned with a square jaw that contrasts with her mouth, which is always restless (and soft). Juan is dressed like a gangster in a grey and white pinstriped suit, a pearl grey tie with exquisite detailing and a starched white shirt (how can he bear it? it's too tight around the neck).

Across from me, María babbles endlessly as I sit by the coffin or in the garden (which was once mine and Juan's garden, and the children's and the dogs' and the cats' – or rather the cat's) or as I read Dostoyevsky, interrupting myself to listen to Juan's opinions on Rogozhin and the idiot prince, each of us sitting in a corner, in a chair or armchair in different colours and textures and even shapes, in front of the unlit fireplace, remembering how quickly the fire burns the banknotes Nastasya Filippovna threw into the fireplace, and her lover Rogozhin, who ends up murdering her (how I'd love to be loved like that, as passionately as Rogozhin or the idiot loved Nastasya Filippovna!), it doesn't matter if they kill me, I think, sitting in my armchair listening to Mozart's Concerto No. 20, Köchel something-or-other, for piano and orchestra (especially the adagio). Our friends talk loudly around us, teasing my overbearing friend, and Juan, monotonously, theatrically, insists on reliving the scene in which Rogozhin declares his love for Nastasya Filippovna and to prove it tosses the banknotes into the fire (no, once again, it wasn't him, it's Nastasya Filippovna who throws the banknotes Rogozhin got for her into the fire, after she'd accepted them from him – him small, dark, bilious, with a perpetual, impertinent, evil, mocking smile) and all his love is concentrated in that gesture, all the love he feels for Nastasya Filippovna: the heart has reasons that reason does not know, Pascal wrote, verbatim. And so I cry: María's tragic countenance opposite me, frozen in the act of uttering the same word over and over, at the edge of the wound, that absurd wound that is life, a heart swollen with bitterness, a heart literally shattered into pieces.

(Someone rescues the banknotes Nastasya Filippovna tosses into the fireplace, they're protected by the newspaper they were wrapped in, so only the first one is burned).

I'm sitting in a corner reading Dostoyevsky, Prince Myshkin enters a house in Saint Petersburg looking for Nastasya Filippovna, who has run away with Rogozhin: his heart is racing, so fast it feels like it's escaping his chest.

On the enormous bed there is a vague shape covered with a white sheet. Myshkin can feel his heartbeat (more than a hundred and fifty beats per minute); it's beating so loudly it frightens him, he thinks it might be heard through the walls. It contrasts with the funereal silence in the bedroom where Roghozhin is sitting, no doubt waiting for him, unsmiling. At the foot of the rumpled bed is Nastasya Filippovna's sumptuous bridal gown. Her diamond necklace glints on the bedside table and one motionless foot wearing a lace and satin shoe peeps out from under the blanket. Did you bring the knife with you all the way to Pavlóvsk? Myshkin asks. No, the only thing I remember, Lev Nikoláievich, is that I took it out of a locked drawer this morning, it all happened between three and four o'clock in the morning. The knife had been there all along, hidden between the pages of a book. There's something odd, though: I stabbed her right in the left breast, several centimetres deep, but there was hardly any blood at all, it wouldn't have filled even half a teaspoon... Yes, I've heard of that, Myshkin replies calmly, though he's trembling violently, I read about that somewhere, it's some kind of internal haemorrhage. Sometimes there's not a single drop of blood.

Rogozhin improvises two beds, and they both sleep next to the dead woman – it's summer, the corpse will soon begin to stink. Rogozhin has covered it with oilcloth and placed four bottles of disinfectant around it (Zhdanov fluid). By the time they are discovered the smell will be unbearable, Myshkin will have become the idiot once more, and Rogozhin will have temporarily lost his mind.

The only thing that comes too soon is your death.

Or maybe I'm not reading Dostoyevsky, maybe I'm just sitting with my legs wide open, playing the cello while Juan accompanies me on the piano (I'm wearing a full skirt now, flat shoes planted firmly on the floor), we're playing Schubert's beautiful, melancholy Sonata for Arpeggione and Piano, I squeeze the cello tight between my legs and pass the bow over the strings, the deep sound is a lament, I look at Juan, his right hand moves playfully over the keys while his left holds the chord. Or perhaps we're not playing, we're not even together – am I alone? am I sitting at the kitchen table that serves as my desk, that grey-green table bearing a red velvet pincushion, a lucky charm of mine, transcribing Juan's compositions onto manuscript paper? Perhaps at this precise moment I am sighing deeply, from the bottom of my heart, perhaps my eyes are brimming with tears (torrents of grief) and now I start really crying (stinging tears), I cry and cry and cry, sobbing now – Nobody, I say hysterically, tears running down my cheeks (they're salty), my heart aching, Nobody, nobody has ever loved me like Rogozhin and Myshkin loved – will always love – Nastasya Filippovna! Tears roll slowly down my face and I swallow them, as María swallows her words – I like the taste of them. I sit motionless, bent over, Rogozhin's (or Myshkin's) wet face in my lap, between my legs – or is it the cello? The strings are hurting me, and opposite me, in close up, that expressive, perpetually open wound – the absurd wound that is life – in my friend's face. I dreamed I was lost. I woke up furious: I don't know who I am. (My blood pressure has gone up.)

I don't want, I don't want anyone to notice I'm crying, I hope María doesn't realise I'm crying! I'd like to drink my tears, to return them to where they came from, I'd prefer not to behave like a woman, an ordinary woman whose heart betrays her, whose blood is inflamed, releasing vapours that escape through her eyes, but no, I couldn't bear it, no, I can't bear it, I've cried so much my tears have dried up, now come on, let's not exaggerate, it's not like I really care, I don't care about anything any more, anything, not my stifled sobs, nor my uneven breathing, nor Juan's body, nor his wispy, stiff (waxed?) moustache, nor his jaw held up by a black handkerchief that exaggerates the sallowness of his face, nor the beautiful clothes tailored in the workshop of a famous designer, I don't care if the pin cushion is heart-shaped and made of red velvet, or if the heart (his heart) has stopped beating, or about the regulation hundred beats per minute, or the story, or the heart that's only a muscle (the centre of life) (if you ingest (small) quantities of (children's) aspirin consistently over a long period of time it can reduce your risk of heart attack by 44%) (that's how I'd like to die, during the night, of a silent heart attack), nor am I interested in talking to my overbearing friend – heavyset like a farmer, or perhaps a butcher – standing now among the elegant ladies who, like María and I, have come to this funeral, and it occurs to me that youth is a divine gift, and I start humming that tango about a dishevelled-looking woman in faded shoes and a brown suit who when she was young and very beautiful used to recite (with her boyfriend) lines of Rubén's poetry (Rubén Darío, I mean, I hope that's clear).

And words acquire a weight when they're written down, after I rest my fingers on the keys, in the silence of the night, only a love like yours has moved my heart that way. I smile, What's so funny, exactly? asks María. Has she seen me smiling or crying? Nothing, I say, a memory, but she's not listening any more, I hope she doesn't realise my eyes are red, my pulse is racing (more than a hundred beats per minute): it would be humiliating, but in truth I know she's not listening (so then what am I afraid of?), nor is she interested in anything except the beating of her own heart (we each have our own little heart). (Opposite me, through the window that looks out onto the patio, I see a squirrel go by as I'm writing this story, climbing the branches of a leafless tree. It's cold, it's the middle of winter. I shiver – if it weren't for its tail it could be a rat). María picks up the thread of her story again, urgently weaving a narrative as absurd as life, an absurd wound. You know, don't you (no, I don't know), of course you do, that everybody loved him, how could they not, so handsome and kind and charming and anyway, I don't know why I'm telling you this. Did you see he grew out his moustache? Of course, I nod, why are you telling me this, yes, I saw that he grew out his moustache, it's wispy, grey, useless, and yes, a long time ago, when we still lived together, he was very handsome. Yes, I know everybody loved him (mind you, my main feeling towards him is resentment, but as the tango goes, resentment, my old resentment, I'm scared you might really be love). And there was me thinking he'd die alone like a dog, I say (the presence of a domesticated animal in the house reduces the effects of stress by up to 50%), there was me thinking he'd die alone like a dog, I repeat very quietly, or maybe loudly, in fact, because this time María pulls a surprised face, It's not me that thinks that, I cry (vehemently), I'm not saying that, his brother used to say so too, yes, his brother used to say that: When he dies, yes, at the end of his life, Juan will be alone like a dog (and dead dogs, as we know so well, don't bite).

Words, words, words, random, meaningless – or are they? They should be meaningful, they're spoken from the heart, unfiltered, even if accidental – and don't they say that words can kill? We end up developing this mortal instinct, a wish to kill, to kill with words, yes, words wound us, wound our hearts, they injure, kill, or at least we would like our words to kill – murder, rather – especially when they're uttered at the pace María utters

27

them, at the convulsive pace of gossip, of macabre funeral
chitchat, with her hypocritical statements – their rhythm
is different from Glenn Gould's rhythm when he played
the Goldberg Variations towards the end of his life, that
period when he only played in studios accompanied by
technicians to help him touch up the final product, the
record that would be sold to music fans, fans who would
mark the galloping pace with their feet, the pace at
which Gould first played Beethoven's sonatas and Bach's
Goldberg Variations, provoking a scandal. A galloping
pace: María and her words, the human heart recognises
them. Scorchingly imprecise words, spoken without
thinking, connections made unconsciously, like when you
unintentionally – or intentionally – fixate on someone's
defects, and then when you actually find yourself talking
to that person, although not always, thankfully not always,
but often, in truth, you reveal, without meaning to (or
meaning to) what you really think, in an allusive phrase
that highlights your own defect, the speaker's defect, by
offending fat people, bald people, short people, hunch-
backs, beggars, thieves, egomaniacs, social climbers, social
climbing mourners (the ones who've come to the funeral
to talk and talk and gossip and badmouth, as people do
at funerals: I had a hunch, someone says, I knew before
it happened, No, another says wearily, I'm telling you,
death doesn't go around whispering in people's ears,
it just comes out of nowhere when we least expect
it), yes, words tend to spill from their mouths without
thinking, straight from the heart – the heart has its own
questionable motives – words like the lyrics to that song
I heard yesterday on the radio: pure heart, broken heart,
a Spanish song by Alejandro Sanz (a former flamenco
singer), a popular song Federica and Corina used to
listen to in the car on the way home or to their father's,
back when they used to visit him. Words spoken, words

spoken from hearts swollen with remorse or anger, hearts accidentally spilled, quick words driven by the unconscious, incoherent, parodic, descriptive, realistic or full of bitterness, words full of the violence of a broken heart, broken not by a heart attack but by rage. Juan, who had a broken heart and couldn't breathe or enjoy anything, is becoming or has become a saint: his sainthood doesn't depend on him still breathing, because neither saints nor angels breathe, they are fantastical beings who come to earth from heaven to honour us; their walk is slow and elegant, subtly rhythmic, like Glenn Gould's hands, or Gustav Leonhardt's, moving over the piano or harpsichord keys as they play, with infinite patience and mastery, Bach's Goldberg Variations.

It isn't unusual, Juan was saying to us one of those nights when we were all together in the living room, which was almost always freezing, where we played or listened to chamber music, or to him, as he told stories in his theatrical (operatic?) voice: No, it isn't unusual, he was saying, for a performer, over the course of their career, to record the same pieces several times, the pièces de résistance of their repertoire. And it's not unusual for those recordings to differ (every performance is different (I think to myself), thus demonstrating the various ways a player has understood a piece as well as their own artistic evolution – sometimes their technique itself changes, their phrasing, their fingering, or, in the case of string instruments, the way they hold the bow): the two recordings we have of Gould playing the Goldberg Variations typify this, separated as they are by twenty-five years, that's right, and being so far apart, they mark the emergence and the culmination of his career. Gould made the first recording in June 1955 and, having always been considered a child prodigy, immediately became the world's most famous international pianist, while the second recording, of one of his last performances, posthumously made him a saint, a myth. The recordings have an important place in performance history because of how incredibly different they are, especially when it comes to their length. Gould explained his theory of slowness in great detail in an interview with Tim Page: I like listening to (and, obviously, playing), he said, any piece of music that really moves me, that touches my heart, at a very pensive, deliberative pace (I call it tempo), and you see, Page – Juan says that Gould said – I used to think the opposite, I thought it was better to play pieces at a fast (convulsive? frenetic?) pace, but as I grew older, I began to have the impression – increasingly so – that many performances – among them, most of my own – are too rushed (for the heart to work properly we have to keep the spirit peaceful: it's healthier to be calm). In truth, Gould insisted, the only music that interests me (without exception) is contrapuntal music; it demands a slow, reflective, regular pace (like a normal heartbeat). And it's precisely this fact, he specified – the lack of respect for that slow tempo – that most upsets me when I listen to my first recording of the Goldberg Variations. Yes, that record had a huge impact, Juan reiterates, sitting as always in the high-backed blue armchair, the rest of us listening (en masse and against our will?) with a glass of tequila in one hand and a cigarette in the other (a Marlboro), the fireplace still unlit despite the cold and Gould's last recording playing quietly in the background. He played the Variations on almost all his concert tours, and then afterwards, when he put a definitive end to his public life as a concert pianist, you could hear fragments in the broadcasts he prepared for a Canadian radio company: to each their own Bach. (I, on the other hand, have a particular devotion to Sviatoslav Richter, both as a pianist and as a man, perhaps even more than to Gould, and so I should say that I do not completely agree with Juan here, although perhaps his view will carry more weight, seeing as he was the pianist and I am a cellist. Richter didn't limit himself to playing a single composer – his repertoire was immense and, as several of his admirers have rightly pointed out, he played Bach with the severity and pleading modesty of a genius, Schumann with the romantic delirium of a man possessed, Prokofiev with a kind of wildness and Liszt with a phenomenal virtuosity, so refined as to be equalled by only Liszt himself (Liszt being one of the great virtuosos of all time); yes, Richter played every composer perfectly and with great respect – he was a protean pianist: Gould was more obsessive and much more arbitrary.)

(We're all drinking, enjoying ourselves, in the living room, the alcohol doing the work the fireplace, warming our discussions and our bodies; Juan, on the other hand, with his scholar's obsessions, does everything he can to freeze our souls.) The decision to record the Variations again was the product of Gould's conversations with another music critic, Bruno Monsaingeon: For me, Gould said, the Variations contain magnificent passages as well as truly dreadful ones (in one of the Thomas Bernhard books I have on my bedside table – I tend to lose patience while reading him – he does something similar, disparaging almost all the great contemporary writers and musicians). (The two pianists could not have more different understandings of music and performance! Richter would play very different pieces with the same passion: he knew how to draw out what was extraordinary about them and, instead of disparaging them, he revered them.) Gould concluded his emphatic observations with this crushing (and presumptuous) sentence: as a work of art, as a concept, which is to say, in their entirety, the Goldberg Variations are a failure (to reiterate, I really do not agree with Gould nor with Bernhard nor with Juan). (The great Romantic composers, the ones Gould disparaged – Schumann, for example – tended to rehearse Bach's contrapuntal works daily using adaptations for the piano by Felix Mendelssohn, a composer Gould admired, although he did not include him or any other Romantic composers – not Chopin nor Schubert – in his repertoire.)

(Gould only played in studios, and at the end of his life he barely travelled, or only from Canada to the US) (in contrast, Richter did many tours, preferring to play in small, forgotten concert halls in the countryside, French granaries turned into improvised theatres, old Austrian castles, ancient Bohemian seaside resorts, libraries in Bavaria and Ukraine, and, afraid of flying, he travelled around in a modest little van, accompanied wherever he went by a beautiful neutral acoustic piano, like a blank canvas (he who, in addition to being a pianist, was a painter), a piano that had been a gift from a famous Japanese music house and which went with him all the way from Moscow to Siberia, from where he set off for Japan) (by boat, naturally).

Gould deliberately avoided using his first recording (sought-after as it was) as a starting point for his second one. He didn't listen to it again until three or four days before he began to record the new one, in the studios in Columbia where he worked and made his most important recordings. A curious experience, he said, it gave me a great deal of pleasure to listen to it, the phrasing gives it a great sense of humour (I like Gould, but he is frustrating (when Juan recounts this scene from Gould's life, it occurs to me that he speaks with the diction of an orator, or perhaps a local mayor), yes, it's true, Gould really was a genius, but he was often vain, overbearing and conceited, and Juan used to become just as unbearable

when he got it into his head to explain Gould's theories).
It's obvious that the young performer, Juan explains, the
one who played the Goldberg Variations in 1955, would
have ended up being just another musician, his concerts
anodyne things, lost in the multitude. From a technical
point of view, Gould repeats, by which I mean if you look
at my fingering, from a purely mechanical perspective,
my approach to the piano hasn't changed that much (I'm
looking at one of the many photographs of him in which
he is still very young, thin, self-assured, with a handsome
head of long, loose hair lifting in the wind, and admiring
his beautiful hands, one of which rests on his hip, showing
off one of his fingers: long, nervous, sensitive) (in another
shot he's very stooped, almost bent double, like an old
man (or was it that his spine was too flexible?) although
he must have been very young in the photo): in truth the
way I play the piano hasn't changed, it's been constant
over the years – static, some of my critics like to say – but
the difference, Juan says that Gould said, is immense –
when I went back and listened to my first recording of
the Goldberg Variations I found it impossible to identify
with the player's spirit; I felt like a ghost had slipped
under my skin, like I'd been possessed by some spirit.
It's so strange to think that that pianist was once me (the
squirrel goes past again, its tail grazing the dry branch
of the tree visible through my window, I interrupt my
writing to watch it, my computer sits on the immense
green kitchen table that serves as my desk, there is a
heart-shaped, red silk pin cushion on it, and the squirrel's
tail is thick and fluffy) (it makes me feel sick) (it's all so
fleeting!). It's an exaggeratedly pianistic recording, and
that is perhaps the greatest reproach I could give to any
performance: it shows off technique and strategy, things
that, in a true pianist, Gould insisted, are entirely dispen-
sable (life is an absurd wound).

What most annoyed Gould about his first version of the Variations, Juan repeats, taking a sip of tequila and a drag on his cigarette, the one from 1955, is the lack of cohesion in the overall structure of the work. (The memory makes me shiver: the way he tells this story is repellent) (or was repellent) (the way Juan tells it, I mean, Juan) (I see that now) (the squirrel never seems to finish running past the window). The thirty modifications to the main theme in the 1955 recording should not result in thirty anonymous miniatures, each with their own individual movement and unique character; on the contrary they should represent the logical development, the organic and intermingled growth of a single, coherent piece. Later, I understood (Gould added, Juan explains) (Juan and (also) Gould (or rather his words) (as relayed by Juan) are still tearing at me) that a piece of music, however long it may be, had to maintain a specific – I was going to say tempo, but that's not the right word – a specific beat, a fixed rhythmic point of reference. While he spoke, Gould was bundled up in an absurd number of jumpers and jackets to stop him from feeling the cold, Juan adds, despite the interview taking place in July, in the middle of summer (Nastasya Filippovna lies on the enormous bed, dressed in white silk; a knife, stained with a single drop of clotted blood, lies next to her body, which is covered with a thick oilcloth to smother the stink: it's high summer in Saint Petersburg (the white nights), there's a bottle of disinfectant placed at each corner of the bed, like altar candles: Rogozhin placed them there before succumbing to a fever. Myshkin has achieved serenity – a true autumnal peace, perhaps, like Gould once wanted to achieve?)

It's plain as day, the pianist explained, that using the same metre indefinitely ends up being deadly boring (meanwhile, if your heart's metre – fifty or a hundred beats per minute – were interrupted, if it were altered too much, you would die). But it doesn't have to be like that, you can take a base beat, set it up on a model that follows a rhythm tied to a subdivision of 2–4–8–16–32, and if it's interrupted every now and then and you use less visible coefficients (we might say less audible coefficients, Juan interrupts), these divisions and multiplications can act as a subsidiary beat in a specific passage of the composition, intensifying its meaning considerably.

I would like, Gould added, in that first interview with Bruno Monsaingeon Juan mentioned, I would like to think that when I play, when I record (especially recently), an autumnal peace reigns, the kind of peace that reigns in rural landscapes seen from my car window, the fields full of scruffy haystacks I pass on the way to this village (me, Nora García) to join the other mourners saying goodbye to Juan. I don't claim to have achieved excellence in my latest performances, Gould concludes, but if I could be sure that with that recording (the last one) we came close to achieving a degree of perfection, not only of a technical but also of a spiritual order, I'd be the happiest man on earth, I would be truly satisfied. (I, on the other hand, although I have reached that moment, the autumn of my life, still don't feel at peace, or maybe I only ever feel an autumnal peace when I have my cello between my legs and I'm playing Bach's solo suites).

Despite the fact that Gould made other recordings before he died (pieces by Brahms, Strauss, Wagner) the second version of the Goldberg Variations (it's important to remember that the first recording, the one from 1955, was made live, at that fabulous concert when Gould all of a sudden became the most famous pianist of the twentieth century) (it's also important to remember that Gould was a child prodigy) represented to some degree his will and testament, the zenith of his artistic wisdom.

As I listen to Juan, I start comparing again, posing the eternal question: what kind of player do I prefer, Glenn Gould or Sviatoslav Richter? Gould's technical ability and immense knowledge of his favourite musicians (though only his favourites), his expressive intensity, his distance, and his strategic ability to confront the market, make him a genius (or so Bernhard assured us), but, at the end of the day, Richter's wise and modest performances (well, sometimes haughty actually) the way he modulated the sharp edges, for example, when he played Beethoven – particularly his late sonatas – marking terrible, sonorous, yet still delicate chords (attacking them with the immense strength of his hands and arms), arpeggios so extraordinary in register only a deaf man could intuit them – make me prefer him. Richter had his own way of disparaging the market – he rejected publicity, maintaining both the grandeur and the modesty of a real artist; he was a conductor who decided to be a soloist (at a time when soloists aspired only to be conductors) or, even better, to accompany soloists (a number of opera singers, for example) or simply to be a member of a chamber ensemble (playing Schubert's trios, or Beethoven's). His hands were magnificent, large, long-fingered, powerful, a little rough, and they spanned the octaves perfectly (not that this matters, there are great pianists – like the small, sickly, Russian composer Alexander Scriabin – who have diminutive hands). Richter played majestically, very upright, his back and arms pulled taut, his feet tense on the pedals. (Fournier notes that the first time he heard Richter, in the Mozarteum in Salzburg, he realised his hands were sweating and his stomach churning – a result, perhaps, of the great pleasure he felt at hearing live a pianist he had admired for a very long time and whose music he had only been able to hear in recordings.)

Sometimes, towards the end of our life together,

when we were alone in the living room of our country house listening to recordings of first one, then the other great pianist, Juan and I would get into heated arguments that often ended in violence. Was it perhaps because of our diametrically opposed ways of seeing the world? I only understood this later (or perhaps I'm only realising now, as I contemplate, with a strange calm, his sallow face, visible through the window of the coffin).

I'm in Buenos Aires, I've just arrived, my name is Nora García: they've invited me to hear a Daniel Barenboim concert at the Teatro Colón. When the pianist comes out, people stand to applaud enthusiastically at length. Barenboim is blonde (or has he gone white? a few wisps of hair are smeared across his skull) and not especially tall; he descends, carefully yet nimbly, a small, red-painted platform (down steps that throw the dilapidated beauty of the wooden stage into relief), wearing a black suit (it's almost, although not quite, a smoking jacket), and gives a friendly, slightly stunned wave; when you look back at some of the images on his album covers it's clear he has lost weight and has aged – there is one particular photo that affects me, in which Daniel, recently married to Jacqueline du Pré, looks happy, with a full head of dark, curly hair; she, on the other hand, has very long, delicate, blonde hair, tied back, a few loose, golden, Gongorine strands flying around her face; her eyes sparkle, her mouth half-open (in ecstasy?), her lips slightly moist; both are dressed in high fashion for the sixties, an era in which making love not war (which still had not finished in Vietnam) was preferable. He looks at her, spellbound, and she smiles happily: so great a happiness cannot last, of course (why does a love so, so intense have to end?); in another photo it looks like they're playing one of Beethoven's sonatas for cello, violin, and piano, along with Pinchas Zukerman: they're staring into each other's faces with that same captivated look (a look that means the violinist may as well not be in the photo), the same ecstasy, the same wretched, predictable future.

People are packed like sardines (as they say) into the Teatro Colón; people standing, sitting on stairs, leaning against the walls of the ground-floor boxes, filling all the interstices between the stalls, the circle, the gallery, and the gods – up there everyone, without exception, is standing, listening to the pianist, leaning on the railings, their heads up near the clouds painted on the ceiling rose fresco, with its antiquated figures in luxurious dress framed in bright blue, like something out of a fairy tale. Above the stage, a papier mâché trompe l'oeil suggests great lengths of cloth hanging above the (slightly dusty) red velvet curtains, which actually only begin halfway down the (very high-ceilinged) theatre, and which culminate in a beautiful band of frieze-like, golden embroidery falling in heavy pleats to the floor. Above the grand piano (a Steinway? does Daniel Barenboim travel with his piano, like Sviatoslav Richter and Benedetti Michelangeli?), and almost the same size (as the piano), hangs a round, red velvet lampshade, identical, except in its proportions, to the lamps that illuminated the dining rooms of wealthy residences in the 1920s, or rather (leaving the rest of the room in modest darkness) illuminated the faces of those who, seated around the table, ate delicately off art deco crockery, silently sipping their soup. The lamp reminds me of the red silk pin cushion I always keep with me (a lucky charm?) as I write (a fetish, perhaps?), placed on the enormous (olive green) kitchen table in the other house, where Juan relates, in his magnificent (perhaps a little exaggerated – operatic?) voice, Glenn Gould's conversations with Tim Page and Bruno Monsaingeon. The curtains framing the stage in the Teatro Colón, and the lamp crowning it, look like they were made with the same sumptuous velvet Scarlett O'Hara used to sew the low-cut red dress with which she seduced Rhett Butler in Gone with the Wind (we're so poor, the man who takes the money says, as we queue for the lift to take us to the fifth floor (he's a tall, elegant, grey-haired, white man, with a masculine face: a prince knocked off his horse?), we have so little money we haven't even been able to buy toilet paper for the bathrooms; the bin men and cartoneros collect rubbish from opposite the theatre, where the bins are protected by a fence, the same type of protection given the streets near the Plaza de Mayo the day after my visit to the Colón: metal bars and an interminable wall of police to stop demonstrators from setting up camp).

Barenboim is playing Beethoven's Sonata No. 13 – he'll give eight concerts in which he will play (from memory) all the (thirty-two) sonatas. His movements are quick, the technique very good, but it fails to move me – I'm much more moved thinking (as I listen to the pianist in the concert hall) about Beethoven, recalling that when he composed that sonata he hadn't yet gone deaf: it's obvious from the exactness of the chords, the clarity of the trills, the fanciful juggle of hands across the piano: the left hand climbs above the right, marking the melody, the arpeggios resounding: Barenboim's left shoe flashes as he presses the pedal: from my seat I can see him front on: when he finishes the sonata's first movement he stops, takes a dark handkerchief out of his pocket and wipes away his sweat, as people shift in their seats and cough as though being directed by a conductor. When silence falls again, he takes up the second movement with brio and the audience members sway in time with the melody and lean back in the balconies to better observe, then close their eyes in ecstasy: when the final chord dies, people stand and applaud furiously: a strong smell of

39

mothballs emerges from the ladies' fur coats, flooding the concert hall with its stink.

Barenboim left Argentina with his parents, aged nine, and returned almost forty years later, and yet, as he himself confesses in an interview in which his Argentine-accented Spanish flows with some difficulty at first, he clearly remembers the smells, the colours, the layout of the buildings and the plazas, the beautiful buildings and beautiful, now dilapidated plazas, on whose corners piles of rubbish are left for the cartoneros, those legions of ragged-looking men, to separate and recycle.

All time, all moons, all blood reaches a place of stillness: the Teatro Colón still retains vestiges of its old nineteenth-century splendour, and there, from one of the seats in the gallery, I, Nora García, a cellist previously married to Juan (who is now dead but was a pianist), am attending a Daniel Barenboim concert in which he will play Beethoven's thirty-two sonatas in the Teatro Colón in Buenos Aires. Daniel Barenboim, a pianist who was married to Jacqueline du Pré, a famous, beautiful English cellist, who died very young wracked by multiple sclerosis, a sly disease (in one of her last records, in which she is still radiant, ecstatic, feverishly embracing the cello (she is playing Saint-Saëns's cello concerto), the traces of illness are already making themselves known in slight imperfections in the way her bow imprints itself upon her instrument's strings).

Is that Juan's emphatic voice again? Is it possible? On 29 May 1981 (a little after midnight), when Gould left the CBC (Columbia Broadcasting Corporation) studios, located at 207, 30th Street, New York (an old Presbyterian church), he brought a chapter of the history of recorded music to a close, as well as the final chapter for producer Samuel Carter, who represented Gould and many other famous artists. Indeed, the Goldberg

Variations was the last record to officially be recorded there: the Columbia Broadcasting Corporation (CBC) – Mecca for all great virtuosos – was to be sold, a victim of the reversals of fortune of an industry that, like any other, had suffered the onslaught of multinationals and international competition. For Glenn Gould and those whose good fortune had for years been linked to the CBC, the old church is a haunted place, said Samuel Carter, as an epitaph for his own company. Juan ends by suggesting that the recording might make Gould another of those (doubtless immortal) ghosts: in the living room, Gould's last recording of the Goldberg Variations can be heard playing very quietly in the background.

Beginning and end meet, as in the esoteric symbol of the ouroboros, the snake that bites its own tail, perfect allegory of the infinite and also of eternal return (we might say wrestling with the angel). An angel whose heart is literally shattered into pieces, only a small part of which remains healthy, a heart broken by disease, not love, a damaged heart (the heart is only a muscle), partially injured, with its one, two, three, four, five bypasses carried out in several emergency operations, acts of salvation, the minor reconstruction of bridges and roads, because the blood is flowing without reaching the river, it's been diverted without purifying the lungs correctly, despite arteries and veins having been reconstructed or cleaned, or new arteries and veins having been implanted bearing new traffic signs to help the blood make its way correctly to every part of the body, the legs, the stomach, the hands, the fingers, the eyes, the nose, the brain but first of all it makes its way, purified, to the lungs – or does it make its way, purified, from the lungs to the heart? A heart aching at the sight of so much misery? I must check whether those roads are winding or straight (every year more than 50,000 people die from heart attacks in

France, and 300,000 in the United States – how many in Mexico?), because they link one place to another, like all roads; but what should be done if the heart is shattered into a thousand pieces, if the mitral valve (or was it the tricuspid?) stops working and there's liquid in the lungs and the bridges over the lakes are collapsing and all of a sudden you're having a massive heart attack? (Men are more likely than women to suffer cardiac arrests) (a thoracentesis to draw fluid from the lungs might be one of the most painful procedures a patient can undergo, perhaps more painful even than childbirth).

During a heart attack, part of the heart dies, leaving only a piece of muscle – a small part of that prodigious muscle – intact, and this provokes anxiety, angst, trouble breathing, moving, climbing the stairs in your home or on planes when you're on tour, because aeroplanes demand that passengers have a whole heart, a heart of steel and not a broken heart with two useless or missing parts (the sciences are now all working together to save this beautiful organ, the organ of life, the organ of feeling, our heart, yes, all the sciences together, chemistry, biology, physics, genetics, engineering): of course, the consequence of a heart attack is that the heart is stripped of cardiac tissue, or split down the middle, like María's face, María's shattered face or Juan's shattered heart, shattered by the heart attack (if these problems aren't attended to immediately – problems of cardiac rhythm – you are less likely to survive; indeed, if there has been no intervention within four minutes of the heart attack, which is to say, if the heart is not restarted, then the brain, deprived of blood flow, will suffer irreversible injury), the heart attack shatters and breaks the heart, leaving only a small section that is healthy but fragile, and this prevents the body from experiencing pleasure, the by now skeletal body, because you're not eating these days and despite everything you keep smoking and smoking and smoking (and drinking, mainly tequila) (Herradura reposado) and despite everything you're dragging an oxygen tank around with you and running the risk of dying from respiratory arrest. Life is an absurd wound, and it's all so fleeting! When a heart sickens it loses its brilliance, the membranes get clogged and an inflammatory serum exudes into the central cavity (in order to avoid this, it's important to have a healthy lifestyle, not eat saturated fats, dress your salads with olive oil, eat walnuts, dates, and almonds, maintain a varied diet, avoid too much salt). That's when the parietal and visceral layers start building up every time the heart beats – and if the heart doesn't beat, the body dies – creating friction in the front part of the chest which can be heard through a stethoscope or even through percussion. (Semiautomatic defibrillators increase the chance of survival from an average of 20% to 50%, in some places they are known as idiot-proof because anyone can use them, all you have to do is press a button that sends an electric shock into the heart and restarts its rhythm – 250,000 pesos, the price of a life!) (Life is an absurd wound!) The heart, that life-giving organ, home to our feelings and therefore our soul, symbol of love, yes, where our life and feelings reside. Initially, cardiac surgery was limited to repairing genetic defects, the majority of which can now be operated on: valve surgery is an important part of this work (they use animal valves, from pigs or cows), as are metal valves. It's important to note that this surgery has its limits and that after eight or ten years, calcification tends to build up and then it's necessary to operate again. The anatomy of the body, and specifically of the heart, takes us back to humanity's great myths, life and death, the origins of humans and their future. Sometimes when the heart's membrane is torn and the lining of its case is broken (the silk lining of my cello case), mechanical functions overlap, the heart atrophies and all of a suddenly you're in cardiac arrest. Is that right?

Is that what happened?

His heart atrophied?

The heart is protected by the sternum, the ribs, and the pericardium: an incision is made in the middle of the thorax, underneath the sternum. They saw through bone (splinters flying) and the pericardium appears, the membrane that surrounds and protects the heart. By now the damaged coronary arteries are visible – another surgeon is preparing the implant (they often use part of the saphenous vein (in the leg), or else a mammary artery is diverted from its normal route). The heart emerges from the thorax, is placed on the sternum (on the right hand side of the sternum): it's difficult to operate on a moving heart; a special procedure known as extracorporeal circulation (using a machine made specifically for this purpose) keeps the heart going and allows blood to circulate around the body (especially to the brain) during the insertion of the implant: one part of the chosen implant is attached to the aorta and another part is placed under the obstructed coronary artery. Once the operation is complete, the heart is returned to its place, its normal movement – the diastole and the systole – starts up again immediately, blood flow is re-established, a vascular bypass has avoided the blockage. After the operation, which lasts from two to five hours (depending on the number of arteries being operated on) (or according to the surgeon's skill) (a single operation can involve up to five bypasses), the patient stays under observation for several days in the intensive care unit, before being moved to a regular ward. That's when rehabilitation begins.

He's going to die alone like a dog, I repeat aloud, when my interlocutor has gone, he's going to die alone like a dog, yes, and dead dogs don't bite, God I wish he'd died alone like a dog, but that's not what's happened, he died in company, like a hero, surrounded by dogs and bitches, men and women and children, he has become an angel, a pure, miraculous being who left his mark on the world, as is evident from these men and women's red eyes, my red eyes, María's red eyes, from these mourners whose hearts are deeply moved: Juan has left a huge void in the nation, a space that's impossible to fill, an immense void in the history of national and international music, he has left his work unfinished, work he did so well – searching out lost scores and manuscripts, going from museum to museum, from music archive to music archive, travelling from Vienna to Berlin and Berlin to New York looking for manuscripts and scores, manuscripts and scores that would allow him to demonstrate in his lectures and books that Bach was different to Pergolesi, the former probably dying peacefully at home, sorting through his notes, composing cantatas, tempering his harpsichord, his well-tempered clavier, on which at night, to distract himself and his family (his second wife and their children) Bach would often play his own Goldberg Variations, composed for a student of his called Goldberg, who also played them every night in the house of his patron, Count Keyserling, a nobleman plagued by insomnia. Pergolesi, on the other hand, died very young of tuberculosis, in his bed, anticipating the Romantic fashion that obliged Schubert to die of syphilis and Schumann to descend into madness. And Bach composed partitas and fugues, cantatas and masses, concertos and choruses, and had children, twenty of them, although by different women – not many women, just two, because the first died in childbirth – he had an unquenchable sexual appetite – his numerous offspring are proof enough of that, are they not? his twenty children? (ten of whom survived). Or perhaps it was just part of the routine of daily life, quiet, impeccable, systematic, composing partitas or fugues during the day, playing them on the organ in the evening, teaching his children, whose voices still hadn't broken, to sing fragments of his own cantatas in the choir (as Bach himself did when he was a child), and at night, yes, at night, at night he devoted himself to conceiving children. Bach, a quiet, normal composer, with a steady, domestic sexual appetite, like the chords in the Goldberg Variations when Wanda Landowska played them on the harpsichord or when, right before he died of a heart attack, Glenn Gould played them on the piano, very unlike the way he played them when he was young and became a legendary pianist overnight, the great pianist who played the Goldberg Variations in two different concerts – one in a public recital at the beginning of his career and the other in a recording studio at the end of it – with completely different tempos: in the first concert he tackled the piece with enormous speed, which is to say, in thirty-seven minutes, allowing him to include in the same recording (the one from 1955) fragments of the second book of the Well-Tempered Clavier as well as a fugue in B minor and another in C major, and the four pieces together only lasted forty-six minutes and eleven seconds! And to think, our heartrate is between fifty and a hundred beats per minute! That the heart pumps out five litres of blood every minute and that there are a hundred thousand veins and arteries through which blood flows around the body! The slow pace, on the other hand, must have been Bach's legacy: Glenn Gould's final recording of the Goldberg Variations in 1981 (a time when he no longer went on concert tours and only recorded in specialist studios – the Columbia Broadcasting Corporation (CBC) – and was soon to die of a heart attack) lasts fifty-one minutes and fifteen seconds, which is to say, fourteen minutes and fifteen seconds longer than the recording that first made him famous! And the harpsichord player Gustav Leonhardt – who thought Bach's Goldberg Variations (BWV 988) were without doubt one of his most extraordinary compositions, written right at the end of his life – plays them at an even slower pace, which is to say, in fifty-four minutes and nineteen seconds! (a hundred beats per minute!). The variations were conceived as exercises in discipline for players and they represent a formidable advance in the canon and the fugue and its variations. Johann Sebastian Bach's family used to delight in listening to him play his own Variation No. 30, which Bach referred to as the quodlibet, Juan explained to me (although I too had read this). It's true that Bach poured nothing but love into the composition of his cantatas, just as he poured nothing but love into the impregnation of his wives, both the first wife who died and the second who survived him – those clumsy wives of composers, Juan used to say with a smile, they had a habit of dying young of puerperal fever. Yes, Bach's children were undoubtedly conceived out of love and passion, Juan explained before his (Juan's) heart began to weaken, the human heart recognises virtue, doesn't it? Isn't the heart just a muscle? And Juan would add: How else could Bach have had such talented children (with his first wife, the one who died in childbirth), celebrated composers whose fame surpassed their own father's during his lifetime? Wilhelm Friedemann, his favourite, the talented but insecure and introverted eldest son; Carl Philipp Emanuel Bach, much more renowned than his own father; and finally, another of his offspring, this time the son of Anna Magdalena, the equally famous Johann Christian Bach, who was fifteen when Bach died. Did he not leave an enormous (divine) gift for future artists: the gift of reading people's hearts?

The heart has reasons that intelligence does not know. For Egyptians, the weight of a deceased person's heart determined their innocence or guilt in the eyes of the supreme court judges. The embalmers would extract the heart from the body, deposit it in a jar, and replace it with a sacred insect (a stone scarab beetle). Medicine has since progressed considerably, especially in the field of angina and heart attacks. If a coronary artery is obstructed, blood flow cannot be guaranteed, nor can sufficient oxygenation of the blood, which is why they now build actual tunnels that work as bypasses. These counteract the process of degeneration, because when the mitral valve, for example, doesn't work, circulation is diverted, taking new artificial routes, which does enormous damage to the heart, congests the lungs and shortens one's life considerably. I imagine that Juan had a sudden wave of nausea that left him feeling completely drained. Perhaps, through a superhuman effort, he was able to prop himself up against the wall of the alleyway he was walking down. The pain must have been unbearable, like nothing ever experienced before (it was perhaps, an irreparable pain). Perhaps he understood that he was lost, that his heart had ripped open and he was going to die alone like a dog. But no, a stranger who happened to be passing came to his aid, calling an ambulance to take him to the hospital where many days later I was to visit him, to see him – very thin by now (his false teeth were too big for him), with his wispy little grey moustache and a stunned look in his eyes, because death really was whispering in his ear by this stage.

At home I always listen to the same Bach record, the Goldberg Variations played by Glenn Gould – his last performance, the one that lasts fifty-one minutes and fifteen seconds. My thoughts drift with the rhythm, a slow rhythm, calm, stubborn, the music arithmetical, crystalline, although that clarity and sharpness are often marred when Gould insists on humming along to the austere melody. I open my eyes: I haven't moved from my spot by the coffin. I stare at Juan's yellowing face, then look away, at the sheet music scattered everywhere, on the table, on some of the chairs. Before, yes, before we separated, Juan was very tidy and had all his sheet music neatly archived in filing cabinets, now it's spread all over the huge living room, by the wreaths and among the flowers, on top of the grand piano (a Bösendorfer with sheet music propped up on the rack) with a cello leaning beside it – did I do that? does it remember at all? does it remember those times we used to play sonatas together, by Beethoven or Haydn, or Schubert's Sonata for Arpeggione and Piano (him on the piano, me on the cello) or when he – Juan – played the Goldberg Variations on the harpsichord? There's a harpsichord in the living room, its open top decorated with idyllic pastel-coloured paintings. There are violins, too, a couple of them – is that a Stradivarius or an Amati? Too many violins for a piano player, I say to myself, stupidly. Flowers, flowers everywhere, on the floor, in the wreaths, in vases, with the sheet music and, despite them all, despite the scent of tuberoses and the heavy smell of altar candles and these memories overwhelming me, battering me, memories I murmur to myself, despite all that I cannot shake the smell of mildew, it's circling me like a halo, like those stubborn shadows, those imagined signs, halos around the heads of saints in paintings and statues.

Poor Pergolesi, on his death bed, Juan was saying with feeling – was it that night, having come home from the restaurant after seeing in the new year, sitting by the cold fireplace in the other house, with that overbearing friend who imitated Rogozhin? or maybe it was Christmas, maybe it was the Año Viejo we were celebrating with a glass of champagne in hand, me in a black silk dress and very high heels, Juan in a grey gangster suit with his top button undone – he died so young, Pergolesi, at only twenty-six, disillusioned with life, not long after his opera, L'Olimpiade, performed in Rome in 1735, turned out to be a spectacular failure. Can you imagine? Juan was saying, can you imagine? he repeated, taking a drag of his cigarette. Finally: recognition, Rome, the capital of art and opera! Poor Pergolesi, he was always dogged by bad luck, Juan went on, and everyone listened, rapt, because he really knew how to tell a story (he'd always tell it his own way, so it sounded like a tale he'd just made up on the spot, though in truth the trick was to reveal the secret lives of his favourite composers – something his research often enabled him to do – which was one of his obsessions: digging around in people's private lives). I read about it in his memoirs that were just published, he says, after taking a sip of tequila, which they found in a castle near Pozzuelo, where Pergolesi was buried, apparently he spent several days rehearsing the opera in the theatre in Rome (La Argentina, it's called) with the singers and the orchestra, an opera into which he had poured all his most intense feelings, all his passion, for wasn't he going to perform it in Rome? hadn't he become a famous composer? That said, he later had to change the composition, thanks to the whims of the darlings of Roman society, the divas and the castrati, and when he did – when he adjusted the score and added special arias to showcase the tessitura of each of the singers – a scandal broke out, fuelled by the conductor and Pergolesi's critics, who were Kabbalists. The performance of L'Olimpiade (the name of Pergolesi's opera, the one performed in Rome, whose libretto was written by the famous Metastasio) is swiftly interrupted by booing, hissing and the flinging of rubbish, before the audience storms out of the opera hall. The musician, inconsolable, his composer's pride deeply wounded, sits at the harpsichord and sinks his head into his hands. And then, just when the theatre is silent and deserted, a bouquet of red roses falls to the stage. Heureux le musicien, so the account goes, and Juan repeated it enthusiastically, heureux l'artiste, happy the artist who achieves such a prize in his lifetime, a bouquet of red roses offered by an anonymous admirer! And yet, Juan goes on, as we all listen, rapt, sitting on the sofas in the living room where his coffin now lies, Pergolesi never recovered (did his heart fail?). Before long, Juan says, pulling on his cigarette (a Marlboro Light now), his glass of tequila in the other hand, just like the rest of us listening to him, like those of us now keeping vigil in his house, Pergolesi dies, heartsick from his own misfortune, he dies in a little town called Pozzuoli, miles from Rome, the capital of art. He dies, of all things, wracked by consumption!

Life is an absurd wound and it's all – all of it – so fleeting!

And this is where the vigil is being held, right here in his living room, I myself am sitting here, holding vigil by the coffin, with María's wounded face opposite me, telling me the story of his death over and over again, Juan's death, Juan who was once my husband and my colleague (my heart, bandoneon, is hurt, by your filthy words, loutish, slurred). It was in this very living room where Juan would rehearse his piano pieces: he'd play a fragment, a few beats, and then stop to pick up his piece of manuscript paper and write the notes on the stave, as perhaps Schubert used to do (and Mozart and Beethoven, Pergolesi, too). Juan could sit for six, seven, eight hours at the piano, playing and transcribing the notes he came up with, like Schubert did before he died of syphilis, that abominable disease. Juan used a Mont

Blanc pen to do his musical notations, except right at the end of his life, when he preferred to use a computer. Computers have changed things, everything is simpler now, on a computer you can automatically write the music for each instrument, you don't have create separate sheets for the violin, the cello, and the flute, and yet when he settled down and was no longer flying around the world like a madman indulging in I don't know how many excesses, Juan used to compose beautiful variations, writing them directly onto the staves, the old way, in the great tradition of Bach and Beethoven (whose scores are full of rubbings out and corrections in jerky, incomprehensible shorthand), compositions written specially for us to play later, together, here, Juan on the piano and me on the cello in my full skirt, my legs open wide, squeezing the cello tightly as though it were an unyielding, hard, inflexible (cruel) part of my body. Yes, at first Juan would write his compositions on manuscript paper, then he started doing it on the computer, because things change and time passes and it's no longer necessary to know how to write music on manuscript paper (as Mozart did, by night, by the weak light of a candle, or Rousseau, copying sheet music to earn a living, one page at a time), it's enough to know how to use a computer, to read music on a digital stave then print it out and listen to your composition via headphones, really. It's an automatic, instantaneous process – that's why, María says, Juan said that if computers had existed back then Beethoven's fate would have been different, Beethoven, that perfect oxymoron, a composer who cannot hear his compositions, or rather a musician who has grasped the ineffable music of the spheres (Gould preferred playing Beethoven's early pieces, the ones he wrote before he went deaf, although many performers believe the later ones to be better, more perfect than those to which

Gould devoted himself) (though Gould did play perhaps Beethoven's most romantic piece: the Moonlight Sonata). Modern science really is, well, modern, and you can now instantly hear the music you compose directly on the computer, yes, instantly, or you can scan music played or composed by others, sheet music transcribed by Bach, Pergolesi, Handel, composers Juan liked, Mozart and Schubert too, especially Schubert, whose impromptus he used to play over and over on the piano.

The heart has secret designs that reason does not know, although in truth the heart is only a muscle, like those in our legs or hands. I see a cello in the living room, not far from the coffin (it's perfect) (is it a Stradivarius? It can't be, that would be too expensive, Stradivarius made hardly any cellos, though many violins) (it's reddish and glossy, with a soft, voluptuous body), alright, it makes sense for there to be a cello, there always was, it is my instrument after all, and didn't I live with Juan for all those years? weren't my heart and his heart one? (a single burning heart?). On the other hand, it doesn't make sense for him to have violins (but why wouldn't it make sense, if he was a conductor?). Flowers, flowers everywhere, on the floor, in wreaths, in vases, on top of the piano, with the sheet music – not on the harpsichord, though, because the lid is open and you can see the delicate, romantic-looking figures painted in pastel tones. A heavy scent is choking me, the smell of tuberoses and altar candles and those memories, overwhelming me, battering me, which I'm murmuring to myself (like Glenn Gould while he recorded the Goldberg Variations in the CBC studios), I cannot, cannot shake off that flowery scent, but mainly the smell of mildew: it surrounds me like a halo, like the halos around the heads of saints in paintings and statues.

I've listened to so much music the last few days, these terrible last days of the year, and I've cried so many painful, bitter tears (black tears), I've cried so much while listening to music that I can't listen any more, I can't bear it, I'm full to the brim with it. I start to weaken, tears closing over me, drawing me deep underground, where the clay rebels. (Juan now has a cross clasped between his hands, over his chest, upon his heart, which has stopped beating) (when in love, or when the loved one is absent, blood ascends in waves towards the heart: the efferves-cence produced by its combustion creates vapours that rise up to the brain and, from there, emerge through the eyes (the windows of the soul), transformed into steam (compare their transparency with the thickness and colour of blood): when the cold of sadness slows the vapours down, a subtle alchemical reaction trans-forms them into tears (this is rightly known in poetry as a broken heart) (in your hands)). There's no doubt about it, I'm going to have to spend several days in silence because my feelings are parched, rumpled, withered and I can no longer revive the sad yet pleasurable sensation of immense, melancholy, tearful tenderness, that violent spasm that moves from the throat to the heart – noble, valiant, vigorous organ, the heart, organ of feelings, organ of passion – an intense emotion that passes through or pierces us, moves us, injuring the heart, making it bleed (open, bleeding wounds of the heart), a feeling I can capture more easily when I hear the miraculous combi-nation of notes in certain passages (but only certain passages) of Bach's cantatas (the series conducted by Nikolaus Harnoncourt) (the sudden change from a major key to a minor one), almost always performed by male voices, countertenors, tenors, basses, but mainly by young boys, either singing in chorus or, sometimes, as happened in Bach's time (his young disciples had to sing the female parts) (women were silent in church), as soloists. It's them, the young soloists, whom I love; I find myself moved by young singers, much more than by the perfect voices of more mature, professional singers. Their sound really does pierce my heart, that ephemeral sound emerging from the throats of young singers in the Vienna, Hanover, or Tölzer choirs, a fleeting voice that vibrates so briefly, during a short lapse, that period when their voices are still pubescent, tremulous and uncertain, intact, before the physical changes that overwhelm us during puberty darken their register. I worship, with (all) my heart and (all) my soul, that slender, high-pitched timbre (crystalline and fragile), that infantile (and therefore angelical) register (their testicles have not descended yet, nor has their larynx settled, as Quignard notes), voices that emerge from a body whose sex is tremulous, naïve, delicate, different to the bodies of men, those hard-voiced creatures of clearly-defined sex, radically different from the young Vienna choirboys who create a harmony (or disharmony) when they strike up a dialogue with mature singers (the bass or the tenor) or when they sing a solo, an aria (voice-breaking is a sonorous disease, the only cure is castration). In this adolescent singing, the feminine rises towards the surface but never quite touches it. The indecipherable voice of boys who sing like boys, their hearts on their sleeves, before a physical change alters their anatomy and their vocal range and transforms them into beings with deep, masculine voices, men, slaves forever to age and sex.

Countertenors, men trained in the art of falsetto, sometimes manage to equal the female voice (though never that of boys). Their voices differ from women's voices, and although they can imitate them there is always hidden, deep down, somewhere in the stomach or the centre of the chest, a powerful trace of maleness. Why are countertenors so determined to sing like women, like children (if only they could), or like castrati (how marvellous that would be!)? Can the strident, forced voices of falsetto singers compete? Yes, I wonder again, why do they want to sing like women? is it out of nostalgia? (a desire to anchor themselves in that intermediate period of their lives before their bodies were entirely subjected to sex or age?). The castrati's huge originality depended on the shape and position of their larynx. Indeed, when a man's voice breaks, his larynx descends like his testicles (the voice goes hand in hand with the genitals) but in castrated men it stays anchored (to their child's physiology) in its original place (even women's voices can break a little, a slight change in the voice) (when the menopause hits?), that's why the castrati's vocal chords stayed closer to the resonance chambers resulting in a brighter, higher range, enormously clear timbre and a greater spectrum of harmonic sounds. Why were castrati so fashionable? Why did they hold such fascination? Why do countertenors today want to imitate them, despite their masculine faces and bodies? Why does their throat produce a female voice? If it were only about poetry or sensibility then countertenors would be enough, regular singers who have spent their whole lives training their voices, learning to modulate them, to sing delicate registers, or violent or heartrending or just plain bold ones, but no, I'm convinced (I would have loved to hear them) that the voices of the castrati were sublime. As a cellist who appreciates the deep, intense sound of her instrument and of the human voice, I prefer to hear young singers performing Bach or baroque musicians, singers who are often inexpert, but who (I insist) should come at the top of the hierarchy, for their voices contain flesh, feelings, spirit, instinct, all things physical and spiritual coming together in a subtle, tacit agreement, just as the blue sky sometimes tints the clouds blue, too. When those little boys sing the arias in a Bach cantata their voices tremble, vibrating just for an instant, an invisible instant, achieving a register that's impossible to equal, piercing both them and us, transfiguring both them and us: they have become incorporeal, angelic beings (even though they sometimes sing out of tune and don't manage to reach the highest notes), they are pure fantasy, like Juan after death, an angel now, illuminating our lives. Yes, that's what the trembling, fragile (asexual) voice of the young singers in Vienna is like when they sing a Bach cantata in chorus, and when they sing solo (their voices eclipsing those of the other singers). And in that moment, the moment I hear them singing an aria or modulating a recitative in their fragile, tremulous voices, though it might be difficult for them to reach those high notes, that imperceptible second, that instant is what moves me, moves me so much that I start trembling or sobbing: to be clear, I'm not trembling or sobbing just because their voices break (although that moment really does merit a sob), I'm trembling with excitement because the voices of the young boys in the choir themselves tremble imperceptibly and underneath that tremor hides their real voice, the one that will define them for the rest of their life, that dark wound that is life. But children's voices are ephemeral, they cannot hold on forever to those delicate, pristine registers. Perhaps they can be preserved, though – rather, they are preserved, they are safeguarded forever (forever?) in the imperceptible groove of a recording, and when we hear that recording we experience the delicious sensation again, the one produced by the sweet, tremulous, angelic, ephemeral voice of those young boys: I'm listening to it now myself, I, Nora García, I'm listening to one of Bach's cantatas conducted by Nikolaus Harnoncourt. Those are the voices that rend my heart, the voices of young boys who, if they keep singing – only if they keep singing – will become tenors, basses, or baritones, which is to say they'll sing the way men who devote themselves to cultivating their voices sing, in deep voices with the range of a tenor, a baritone, or a bass, but they will never, ever again achieve the delicate female range they achieved as boys, when their hearts could still be read like open books, their true hearts, broken, in our hands. Or perhaps – why not? – nostalgia for that voice obliges them to become countertenors in order that their bearded, masculine faces might utter sounds that recall those they made when they were children, in that fragile, earlier voice of theirs, sometimes perforated too soon by the prophetic register of manhood.

In one of those get-togethers with friends (were we never alone?) in this very same (enormous) living room in the country house where we're holding vigil over him, me poorly dressed in trousers and boots and a jumper that's too thick, or dressed up in a low-cut black dress, lace stockings and high heels (in the living room of the other house, the one in the city, the fireplace empty in winter), Juan recounts an anecdote from the life of Rousseau, an anecdote from his youth, when he was secretary to a French ambassador in Venice. One day, Rousseau (before he retired from the world, before he began to make a living by copying music one page at a time), Rousseau, I'm telling you, or rather Juan was telling us, Rousseau hears some little orphan girls singing in an orphanage in Venice, teenage girls who sang like angels, and wants only one thing: he will meet those orphan girls, even if has to contravene the rules of the convent; a friend stops him. You'll only be disappointed, he tells him, and you might end up regretting it. Nonetheless, Juan repeats, nonetheless, Rousseau insists on meeting them, on seeing them with his own eyes, those eyes that would be eaten by worms, the same way Juan's eyes, once he's in his grave, will before long be eaten by worms. And of course, what his friend predicted does in fact happen: when he has them in front of him, face to face, when he sees them, none of the girls matches up to her voice: one has a face scarred by chicken pox, another has only one eye, the one at the back is a dwarf, and the last is incomparably ugly, but when they sing behind the choir, hidden by the latticework, they have the voices of angels, yes angels, and angels really are wholly beautiful, both in body and in soul, yes, the orphan girls that Rousseau visited were like angels when they weren't visible, when you could only hear their song behind the latticework, girls who sing (or sang) like the boys sing or sang in the Vienna, Tölzer or Hanover choir in that recording I'm always listening to, a recording in which the register of a voice has been preserved for eternity, trapped in an ineffable moment when the young singers still sang like angels, like the cherubim with deformed faces who Rousseau wanted to meet: the angelic voice of the young Tölzer singers has been preserved forever in the miraculous technology of an ordinary, run-of-the-mill CD, a voice identical in its androgyny to those of the orphan girls Rousseau met.

The first movement of Piano Sonata D 850 in B flat major is very impetuous and impulsive, which is unusual for Schubert, Juan explains, warming to his new (musical) theme, that Christmas or New Year's Eve, sitting in the enormous living room drinking champagne and smoking around the empty fireplace (even though it's freezing), as our overbearing friend dozes off, the one who feverishly repeated Rogozhin's theatrical gesture of flinging banknotes into the fireplace – one that was actually lit – in a wealthy nineteenth-century Russian home, a scene masterfully described by Dostoyevsky and which Juan so loved to recall (although he changed some of the idiot's scenes). The rhythm of the main theme in Schubert's Sonata in B flat major, Juan points out, sitting in the high-backed blue armchair and loosening the light grey silk tie digging into his neck, that theme, he says, dominates the whole piece, with each variation emerging from the previous theme: Juan pauses in his tale, makes a theatrical gesture with his right hand, places his glass on a little table next to him, lights a cigarette (still a Marlboro Light), takes a drag and then, after a masterful, almost pianistic silence, picks up his glass again, stands (his suit is anthracite grey cashmere with fine white pinstripes) and resumes his tale with that implacable, infallible logic so characteristic of his conversation: Schubert modulates some curious chords that suddenly reappear at a much slower tempo (the manuscript reads: capriccioso, in the composer's own hand). And when you get to the central theme the chords from the first theme undergo an impressive transformation, Juan explains, and Schubert chose to use a strident blast of a horn, but on the piano (a remarkable idea, impossibly refined), a real call to the hunt that returns in the coda in much more hurried fashion than elsewhere in the movement. There is a melodic theme – brief as anything – that counterpoints the slow movement, Juan notes, speaking very quietly, it transforms and adopts a syncopated rhythm, lighter, much lighter, angelic, then rounds off with a series of syncopated chords that fall apart, thus creating a harmonic sequence so bold as to be almost Wagnerian, which suddenly fades again (just like that), letting out a sigh so infinitely pained it seems to come from the very depths of the heart. When the main theme is taken up again, Juan says, getting up and heading for the piano, the Bösendorfer – yes, it has to be the Bösendorfer – to show us how the pianist's right hand picks out the main theme while the left plays the part of a violin or viola da gamba, like a basso continuo (played on the cello), letting the piano create sounds known in music jargon as portamenti or expressive glissandi, very Romantic (completely different to those moments of autumnal peace Gould achieved in his performances). When Juan plays the fragment again you can hear the contrast clearly, an impetuous but after all very intimate theme, with a resonant intimacy that untethers a feeling of intense happiness in the depths of my heart that is both painful and pleasurable. This passionate piece that Juan so enjoyed playing surprises the listener, despite the modesty and innocence of the rondo theme – its delicacy is surprising, yes, and that delicacy balances the decisive rhythm of the previous passage. Schubert is undoubtedly both delicate and reckless, and this was always very clear when Juan played him, and is clear to me, now that Juan has died, when I listen to this recording of András Schiff performing that same piece, on this CD with a green cover. Only those two – Juan and Schiff – managed to get the notes to fade gradually as the sonata slowly comes to an end, its rhythm soothing the inconsolable and allowing tears, from the depths of our hearts, to spill slowly, sweetly from our eyes.

András Schiff, for his part, explains something unusual and worth noting: it's only recently that Schubert has begun to gain recognition as a great piano composer rather than just a writer of lieder: Juan understood this perfectly, long before we bought any records by Schiff, a pianist who has become fashionable only since his death (Juan's death). Some of his (Schubert's) other piano pieces were rarely ever played. Juan used to compare them to Bach's Well-Tempered Clavier or The Art of Fugue or Beethoven's thirty-two sonatas, musical monuments, brilliant, incomparable additions to the history of music and art. Juan felt that Schubert's piano pieces were as important for the piano repertoire as Chopin's work (or Lizst's) and even, though perhaps to a lesser extent, Schumann's, a fact long overlooked, so much so that several of Schubert's piano pieces weren't heard until long after his death, his early death from syphilis. Juan assured us – playing the same fragment from Schubert's Sonata D 566 on each of the pianos, which is to say, first on the Bösendorfer and then on the Steinway – that it was a sacrilege to play Schubert on a Steinway, which, though no doubt a marvellous instrument, was (perhaps) too matter-of-fact for those delicate sounds, and so he (like Schiff) recommended·an Imperial Bösendorfer, the same piano I can see from where I'm sitting now, opposite me, in the enormous living room in our old house, as I hold vigil over Juan's body, the body of the pianist, composer and conductor with whom at one point I shared both my romantic and my musical life. Yes, in that living room (along with the sheet music on the music stand) there is a Bösendorfer to be admired, an instrument which, Juan would repeat ad infinitum (illustrating his point with several chords from Schubert's posthumous impromptus), has much more refined and expressive acoustics than a Steinway or a Petrof – yes, if you want to play the work of the Viennese composer (whom we so often played together, especially the Sonata for Arpeggione and Piano, adapted for cello) with sincerity and mastery, you have to play it on a Bösendorfer. Music played on a Bösendorfer achieves a better tonal quality, which the famous, unfortunate Viennese composer's piano pieces demand. No, there's no doubt about it, you cannot play Schubert on a Steinway, Schubert only sounds the way he's supposed to sound on a Bösendorfer. (Speaking of which, where is the Steinway?) To underscore his claim, Juan would interrupt himself in the middle of a chord to go and put a CD (with a green cover) by András Schiff in the (Sony) CD player. It was on a Bösendorfer piano that Schiff played Schubert's posthumous sonatas (D 566, D 784 and D 850), written shortly before the composer died, in the flower of his youth, a year after Beethoven died and Schubert took part in the enormous procession, raising a torch in his right hand and feeling each peal of the Vienna Cathedral bells resound in his heart – the city's way of saying goodbye (with much emotion and solemnity) to the deaf man from Bonn, that extraordinary teacher (Schubert's, Schiff's, and also Juan's).

If I'm not mistaken, it was at an Arturo Benedetti Michelangeli concert at the Royal Festival Hall in London: the concert hall was full, an Englishman whose name I don't remember was conducting – he might have been famous – and the piano was a Bösendorfer brought over specially from Italy by Harrods, as the programme proudly stated. We've flown from Amsterdam; the Italian pianist is one of Juan's favourites, and he's especially keen to hear how he plays Beethoven's Concerto No. 5. Michelangeli is one of the world's most enigmatic and capricious pianists, whose concerts are often cancelled on account of his demands, his moods, and perhaps also because he was Mussolini's pilot in the Second World War, so he hasn't exactly covered himself in glory, except when it comes to how he plays the Romantics, his prodigious and infinitely varied fingering, the contrast between his hands and face, his elegant, delicate phrasing. The pianist's hands run over the piano and are reflected in the instrument's lid, his thin, nervous fingers vibrating, trembling, modulating; he is dressed entirely in black, in a cashmere turtleneck jumper, and has a white handkerchief with which he wipes his forehead; his movements are quick, dry, arrogant, he raises his thick left eyebrow, his neat, straight hair gleams slightly, and a fine moustache lies over the thin, certain line of his mouth. The conductor waves the baton hesitantly, nervously, cowed by Michelangeli, who ignores his movements and forces him to change the rhythm, to follow his own rhythm – he's conducting from the piano, his smile glacial and polite, the smile of an English duke whose face is marked by precisely-inflected vowels, arrogant consonants, and a disdainful, perpetually stiff upper lip. The final chord has barely sounded when the immediate, interminable applause begins, the audience on its feet and shouting, practically howling; the conductor applauds fiercely, flustered, sweating. Michelangeli, tall and thin, bows slightly, leaning on the piano. The conductor: an Italian aficionado who played a Puccini aria to seduce a lady in the street.

Arturo Benedetti Michelangeli gave another extraordinary pianist his start both in music and in life: Maurizio Pollini.

Juan looks at me, strokes my face with his hand, takes me by the arm and we head for the airport, for Glyndebourne in England, where we'll attend the annual opera festival and hear (and admire) Handel's Xerxes: the main role is played by a famous countertenor, David Daniels, a man with a masculine face and the voice of a mezzosoprano.

(...in the middle of the recording of an Emil Gilels concert, while he's playing Schubert's posthumous impromptus, you can hear people coughing: it was impossible to avoid them as the recording was live. In Gould's recordings there's no interference from the audience – he always recorded in Columbia's studios in New York or Canada, and although he demanded the final version be perfect (and edited it like a film to ensure impeccable sound), Gould could never help humming along, a murmur that invariably accompanies the melodies of the pieces he recorded. Fans of Gould have no choice but to listen to the recordings with that irritating sound, a kind of clearing of the throat. When he plays, he imposes his style of playing on us, and his humming is an inevitable part of that style, a style which, despite everything, is, for some music fans (Thomas Bernhard), a sign of his genius, that quality of execution that places him much higher up the pecking order than other virtuosos (in Bernhard's opinion, a celebrated pianist like Brendel is a mere fraud beside Gould).)

There's no order or beauty in this living room any more, the papers are scattered in boxes, on shelves, there's sheet music on the chairs and propped on the Bösendorfer rack: didn't that sheet music, so clearly copied and arranged, show Juan to be a decent, respected man, a hero of the profession, a role model for the vocation, a magnificent pianist and extraordinary composer, a careful researcher, a man of heart? A man, in sum, who the day he dies will, like Beethoven, go with (be accompanied by) thousands of anonymous people and also by friends, real friends, showing the world he wasn't going to die alone like a dog (nor indeed like poor Pergolesi, who died lame at the age of twenty-six – yes, lame, because as well as having tuberculosis Pergolesi was lame). Pergolesi, a musician admired both by Juan and his contemporaries, but disparaged in Rome by music lovers and other composers who, out of envy, hounded him and then, after his death, reworked his arias and were met with roaring success in all the theatres of old Italy. Unlike Pergolesi, Juan was very popular while he lived, although he probably wasn't as great a composer. People follow Juan, everyone followed him; yes, Juan was recognised during his lifetime (the absurd wound that is life) and friends were always coming to visit him, the same friends who have come to bury him, friends who fall apart as he is lowered little by little into his grave, an empty grave prepared in advance, which will be filled once we've heard the speeches, the weeping, the church bells from the convent tolling in our hearts, the shuddering breaths, the vile suspicion, the squeaking of the coffin as it's disturbed, and four men straightening up before sprinkling holy water on his body, holy water that looks like it's come from some filthy puddle, and then someone, I don't see who, flinging a large white flower that falls onto the rough-hewn, white pine wood coffin and then I remember – how could I forget? – that rose or bouquet of roses that fell to the stage as Pergolesi was crying over his failure. And then the bouquets of flowers begin to fall, flowers and more flowers, gladioli, white roses, red roses, yellow roses, Peruvian lilies, carnations, daisies, calla lilies, stars of Bethlehem, tuberoses. Some flowers are fresh, others wilted, and their scents mingle with the scent of the altar candles that people in the procession are carrying (hot wax drips, spills, burns hands) and the tuberoses – especially the tuberoses – whose cloying scent briefly blots out the smell of mildew that has followed me from the house and which, pausing whenever I do, surrounds me like a halo now as I wait at the edge of the grave for them to bring the body. The sun is blinding me; I put my dark glasses on, because neither the sun nor death will let you look straight at it (with impunity).

We've come all this way from the house to the graveyard, a cemetery nestled in the valley, and during the entire procession the smell of flowers and altar candles hasn't managed to mitigate the dirty smell of mildew that's hounding me, flooding me – perhaps I'm the only one who's noticed it, perhaps it's only pursuing me. (Would the smell of Nastasya Filippovna's stabbed body have been mitigated by the four bottles of disinfectant? Four unstoppered bottles of Zhdanov fluid, Rogozhin explains to Prince Myshkin.) And people look on, distraught, their hearts destroyed, nobody is telling jokes any more, like they were in his garden, in my old garden, as the mourners drank their tequilas, and now they're standing by the grave, and the mariachis have fallen silent and the people who gave solemn speeches have also fallen silent and are standing very seriously by the grave without shedding a single tear, because shedding tears is for women. All you can hear is children and old women sobbing (wiping their noses on their smocks) and stray dogs barking. And Juan, Juan has not died like a dog (a stray?) (like the stray dog in his house that died giving birth, wrung out, her dark nipples drooping to the floor?), no, he has died like a hero, he has become a thin, shrivelled angel, wasted by disease; his heart has shrunk, he's lost muscle mass, there's barely anything left on him, his breathing became difficult and he needed an oxygen tank just to walk, his quality of life changed, he couldn't go out so much at night, couldn't travel any more, or research, or give lectures in his theatrical (operatic?) voice, he couldn't live for the moment, live fast, live without giving a damn about disease or pain or even death, with his tainted heart, a heart whose motives were not especially virtuous, a perpetual outpouring of strength and libido, an open, immediate desire, vile suspicion, polymorphous, perverse suspicion (that's how psychoanalysts describe the Marquis de Sade, whose libido was an immense and polymorphous perversity), like the figure in the artwork I'll later receive as a gift, done in strong, simple pencil marks, in which a man can be seen, spreadeagled, his member swollen and immense, the very image of desire, a pure, almost philosophical erection, Heideggerian, if you will (seeing as we're getting philosophical), and next to the man with the excessively large phallus are drawings of other men and women, much smaller in stature, more sickly looking, the recipients of his erection, mere depositories for a desire whose flesh is outsized and whose pleasure is exaggerated, a grotesque, almost ominous scene, but fascinating in its brutal, carnal vitality. And it's nothing more than a few pencil marks, a sketch of a figure with his legs open, equivocal, with proliferating sexual organs, an enormous penis emerging implacable, impeccable, a figure seen inserting one end of his sex into that of a much smaller woman lying on her back with her legs open, while another woman admires, open-mouthed, the sexual activity exposed so plainly in a few pencil lines. You might say, though, that the drawing is incorrect, the artist's name is written backwards, as though he was either out of his mind drunk or indulging himself by depicting a scene in which his whole body has become a long phallus, a single long shadow, as long as the shadow in that José Asunción Silva poem: what remains. And the dick, León Hebreo says in his Dialogues of Love – León Hebreo doesn't mince his words, he says it like it is, without fear of being vulgar – in the impeccable, genuine version by the great writer and chronicler Inca Garcilaso de la Vega, son of an Incan princess and a soldier who was in turn descended from another great poet, the dick, I write, borrowing León Hebreo's words, which Juan used to read to me, sitting by the empty fireplace in the other house, not lighting it despite the cold, the dick, Garcilaso says that León Hebreo says and Juan repeated and now here I am transcribing, the dick is comparable to the tongue in terms of its position, its shape, the way it lengthens and shrinks, its location in the middle of the body and the middle of the picture; because just as the dick engenders bodily creation by its movement, the tongue engenders spiritual creation; and the kiss is common to both, inciting the one to the other.

And I remember his kisses, the taste of his tongue, I, Nora García, and she, Nora García, remembers and cries, or rather she sheds a few tears that she discreetly wipes away – unlike the men who cannot let their tears spill because it wouldn't be manly – although she hasn't brought a handkerchief that would allow her to cry elegantly, dabbing delicately at her eyes, rather she's using a plain old tissue, a tissue instead of an embroidered handkerchief, one that Juan perhaps gave her many years ago or that I – she, Nora García – gave Juan, a handkerchief with his initials embroidered in fine white cambric that she, Nora García, has hidden (I have hidden) among the love letters he wrote to me. And Nora, I repeat, Nora too has cried – I cry like Mary Magdalene herself when they listen to my chest, when they examine me, do tests on me, for fear that in my future or her future – Nora's – there might be a tumour they'll have to cut out, only for her to die ominously, alone like a dog or, to be more precise, like a bitch. Isn't Nora García arguing, isn't Nora García arguing with the dead man? Arguing with he who is no longer the man he is, nor the man he was, he who is no longer Juan, who cannot be Juan – vain shadow – because his body, this body that was once his, is already being eaten by worms?

In a Caravaggio painting of a concert, the performers hold instruments in their hands, touch their fingers to the strings of a guitar, a lute, a theorbo, a cittern or a mandolin; one hand holds a bow over the bridge of a violin, or a viola da gamba bow; the mouths of the figures in the painting open to blow into the mouthpiece of a transverse flute, a trumpet or an oboe, and as the characters play – all of them young, that era of vitality frozen at the precise, stubborn moment in which they are playing their instrument – you can see the slight tremble in their faces, the flicker of eyelashes, that incipient expression (the beginning of silent ecstasy?), an absorbed but glowing look, the look, the flicker of eyelashes, the tremble accompanying each performer's movements, for example the almost prepubescent castrato playing an enormous archlute, a character often seen in Caravaggio's paintings, a young man who as a child once sang in a choir at a school for orphans where future castrati were recruited, so their voices could forever replace the voices of children. Can we read in his gaze what he feels in his heart? Do his eyes, the expression on his face, the shape of his mouth, reveal the truth? Does my mouth, when I play the cello or Juan's when he played the piano? Do the faces of the young musicians painted by Michelangelo Merisi da Caravaggio? Can a castrato express himself sincerely? Aren't the eyes the windows of the soul? Can María's pain be read in that mouth that disappears as she speaks? Can a mutilated face tell the truth? How can we truly be sincere if the organ that produces sounds is not visible? Or the organ that produces colours? Are they real, the harsh colours Caravaggio managed to depict in his paintings, struggling with a lantern that alternately illuminated his models and threw them into shadow, those young people with their clear, faltering voices, their rosy-cheeked, angelic yet still wicked faces? If you are insensitive to others' pain, unable to feel goodwill, your heart will turn to stone – but God can save us by giving us a spiritual transplant. Everything about the castrati's appearance was angelic, Juan explained that same long night before New Year, explained after telling us other stories, including the one about the deformed girls in the Venetian convent that Rousseau once heard singing. Didn't they dress little eunuchs up like angels to hold vigil over dead children in Neapolitan conservatories? The castrati were perfectly suited to the aesthetic ideal of the time – the eighteenth century – across almost the whole of Europe: they were objects to be contemplated, venerated, equated with angels, linked with the traditional figure of winged musicians, thus embodying (much more through their voices than through their actions) purity and virginity. In church, thanks to voices that seemed to challenge the laws of physics, the castrati represented a privileged connection among God, music, and men. Who hasn't used the word 'angelic' to describe Allegri's Miserere, a piece written by a castrato to be sung by other castrati? And finally, weren't they the most perfect expression of baroque art – sculpture, painting, music – representing angels, that most symbolic of baroque figures? There is a contradiction in the German language when it comes to the word alto, used to describe contralto voices. Alt also means old, but boys, girls and women didn't need to have reached maturity to sing alto or contralto parts. The word derives from the Latin alta, meaning high or piercing voice, and we might use the words elated, ecstatic, jubilant to describe soprano voices: a true contralto voice can be characterised by its warmth, its exuberant luxury and above all by its colour, whose radiant tones become dark and velvety – this is how María talks, and I listen in fascination as, sitting next to me, in that chair by the coffin, she describes, enthusiastically and in great detail, the expressions that accompany death.

Among the countertenors who have come on the market, most from English church choirs turned soloists, there is one exception: René Jacobs, partly because he is from Belgium, but mainly because he has managed, by going beyond sacred (internalised) chanting, to find vocal art that expresses great dramatic intensity, the glory of seventeenth- and eighteenth-century castrati. Blessed with a voice that reaches from the top of the mezzo range to the bottom of the chest register and which always retains, even in the lyric repertoire, its masculine timbre, he tackles the virtuoso castrato parts of baroque operas and the simple, intimist music of more recent years with the same ease and perfection.

The genius castrati reigned as absolute masters of eighteenth-century Italian opera and whipped up the public's enthusiasm – their utter devotion, really – beyond the world of opera. Falsettos, though they travelled all over Europe, were no longer in vogue, despite predating the castrati, because they sang exclusively in their head voices – those crystal clear and sometimes imperfect masculine voices.

It would be an exaggeration to claim that, except for in England, the arrival of the castrati determined the fall of the falsettos as soloists in the secular repertoire. Often, even in Italy, many falsettos passed themselves off as castrati, and were discovered when they had children, thus proving they were not eunuchs. In England, castrati and falsettos openly exchanged roles, taking on the same parts as female contraltos. Handel exploited this inter-changeability when he composed parts for his oratorios, choosing the singers depending on the circumstances. Fortunately, Handel wrote his castrati compositions for mezzosopranos. Eighteenth-century opera and theatre complained more and more about vocal cross-dressing and the increasing number of artists able to play both male and female characters. This situation often lent itself to comedy – on one occasion, after twice changing his character's sex in a single scene, the English counter-tenor George Mattocks sung the part of Achilles while dressed as a woman. The mise-en-scène was a deter-mining factor. Most castrati were treated as though they were Greek gods. Female singers, extraordinary though they were, never had the voice or stature to rival them (despite the make-up, heels or platformed shoes and suits). Basically, their voices didn't have the same impact as the piercing, masculine voices the castrati had retained and enriched despite their emasculation. Today, as in the eighteenth century, the voice of a countertenor like

David Daniels is probably the closest thing you'll find to a castrato.

I wander around the garden again, lost in thought, haloed by the smell of mildew and the sound of words brought to me on the wind, words I can't decipher; the words ricochet, resound, engrave themselves, originating from several groups scattered around the space, jumbled, confused. Eventually I hear some words clearly, uttered theatrically, with rapid diction – they're getting closer, approaching me, I can hear them now very nearby, they belong to a woman standing in the middle of a group, with a glass (of tequila) in her hand, a well-dressed woman, sober and elegant, her trouser suit by Emmanuelle Khanh a dark grey colour, or perhaps a brown so dark it looks black – or is it cherry? (Shops exist because vanity is immortal.) She's seen me now, María abandons her friends and hurries over to meet me, and as I watch her approach, cigarette in hand – she's still a way off – from afar she modulates her beautiful voice, hurriedly repeating those well-worn words (as she modulates her sombre voice, it reminds me of an English countertenor, David Daniels, the singer whose voice – I imagine – is the closest thing you'll find to a castrato; the lightness and flexibility of his timbre set it apart from male voices; it also differs from the voices that emerge from women's throats because of its brightness, purity and power; and it is superior to children's voices because of its fully developed adult musculature, its technique, and its expressivity), María's words piece together in great detail the story of his death, the story of Juan's death. Her face is still intact, her features visible, her eyes (I hadn't noticed before) a strange colour – the colour usually described in novels and poems as glaucous (or are they dark as oblivion?) – her nose is slim yet prominent, her face smattered with freckles that are only just visible through her make-up which is darker than her actual skin, her lips are red, outlined with a darker pencil, crimson, almost black, like her cherry-coloured designer trouser suit, probably by the French designer Emmanuelle Khanh, who is practically unknown in Mexico. Her teeth are very even and white, her tongue is pointy (what other shape of tongue could a talkative woman have?) (Juan had lost all his teeth and struggled to talk: those long stories he used to tell in that voice of his, so loud and operatic, casually relaying conversations between Glenn Gould and Bruno Monsaingeon). María is elastic, her gait agile. He couldn't even breathe, breathe, breathe, she repeats, the oxygen tank, oxygen tank, everyone respected him, admired him, he was so handsome, he spoke so well, he was so wise, then he grew that moustache, a wispy, grey, uneven (waxed?) moustache (she's shouting now, everyone is turning to look at her): he was such a good pianist! So charming! So handsome! And he wound up unable to breathe! breathe! breathe! breathe! (The heart is only a muscle that irrigates the body). Her lips, blood red (like the blood that has stopped circulating around Juan's body), disappear bit by bit, leaving a thin, gummy trace, a brief and sinister scar, an absurd wound, life. Hypnotised, I'm barely taking in her words, nor those of the people around us — around me — everything, everything, everything disappears, nothing, not the noise nor the mariachis' tuneless singing nor the trumpets' colourful racket, nothing can detract from the impressive lustre of her voice, which resembles, I've figured out, the voices of the castrati.

María continues unperturbed, recounting scenes from his death. I concentrate, managing to take in a complete sequence, a sequence that María bulldozes with her metallic, nasal voice. His trouble breathing, María says, meant he had to stop in the middle of a concert, and

would get out of breath if he walked too quickly. One
night he felt a pain below his sternum, grinding away
at his chest, that left him first hot then cold, a pain that
also made him wheeze slightly. Later he started to feel
faint and then a savage pain shot through his chest, and
his arms and legs went numb, so he decided to call an
ambulance. He was alone and didn't tell any of his friends.
He spent several weeks in the hospital, totally alone (and
toothless by now), or perhaps visited by some of his
closest collaborators. (Hooked up, no doubt, to a number
of machines whose various wires wove together on the
floor and walls, tracing their epileptic journey, arryth-
mia's deranged design, on strategically situated, different
coloured screens: the uneven beating of his heart). María's
breathing has become laboured with sadness as she tells
this story: in the hospital, she says, he started spitting out
this viscous substance and his pulse became irregular,
so the doctors decided to perform open-heart surgery
on him (the Aztecs believed that human sacrifice, that
ancient, primitive practice that prefigured modern heart
surgery, was necessary for their very survival).

María interrupts herself to wave a woman over, a friend
who greets her, greets me; she stares at me (rude) with one
of her eyes, the other one blind, the pupil obscured by a
whitish cloud. Wow, I say to myself, this is less a funeral
and more a circus, or curiosity shop, or museum, or even
– why not! – a fashion show. The one-eyed woman is
also very elegant: she isn't wearing a patch, her bright eye
contrasts noticeably with the cloudy one – you can't see
its pupil or perhaps I should say that the pupil doesn't let
the light in; that opacity, I think, limits the expression of
truth to a single eye, and aren't the eyes the windows of
the soul? Or perhaps this woman would tell the truth
with neither eye, perhaps – a banal association that has
just occurred to me – it's her veiled eye, her cloudy eye,

that better reveals or shows the truth. Does open-heart surgery reveal the heart? How can we know if the love others show towards us is sincere? Music doesn't lie, we know that perfectly well – we feel it, there's no two ways about it – we feel when a musician plays a piece well (I wonder if it's possible to read a score with only one eye?), we know they're playing with feeling, they're playing with the most authentic passion, a piece for piano or cello or whatever instrument, or for voice, although I prefer talking about the instruments I know best, the ones Juan and I played together, he on the piano and me on the cello. Let me repeat, reiterate: in my opinion, when somebody plays a piece of music well we can tell they're completely sincere, we know because they've transferred their own feelings to the instrument, thus translating the composer's feelings, or what the player believes to be the composer's real feelings; it doesn't matter if those feelings have already been expressed quietly or tempestuously, slowly or convulsively, like, for example, the way Glenn Gould played the Goldberg Variations by Johann Sebastian Bach when he was very young, in only thirty-eight minutes and twenty-seven seconds, or when the pianist Sviatoslav Richter (who won his first music competition at the age of thirty) (completely different to Glenn Gould both in his musical trajectory and how he played the piano) played an immense musical repertoire to perfection, quite different from his contemporaries, or when someone like Mstislav Rostropovich plays Marin Marais's Follies at lightning speed on the cello – Marais, a French composer who wrote for an instrument similar to the cello: the viola da gamba. We know, we intuit that their feeling is genuine, it's clear from the sound, the extraordinary melody the player wrings from their instrument; we know it too when somebody cries – though do we really know? Do we? Tears, a clear manifestation, assuming they are real (how can we check?), of absolute sincerity. And if they are, if the tears are sincere (rather than crocodile tears, as they say), yes, if they're real then tears go beyond words – words, an apparently faithful reflection of feelings, yet capable of betraying them and of distorting reason. In that intangible course that makes visible, or rather audible, the movements of the heart, feelings are falsified and become deceptive, a rhetorical deception. Is it impossible to express passion? How do we overcome the barrier imposed by our own bodies? How do we achieve that, if the heart is just a muscle? How do we see or touch what the heart feels? The broken heart in your hands? My heart was inside his, his heart inside mine.

Juan wrote his compositions and played them on the Bösendorfer (Schubert played on a Bösendorfer too, in the final years of his life, when he was already very sick, but before he was cooped up in hospital, hollowed out by syphilis). Juan composed beautiful pieces in the great tradition of Bach and Beethoven, compositions originally written specially so that he and I could play them together, in the living room where we're now holding vigil over him, Juan sitting at the piano and me playing the cello, wearing a full skirt, my legs wide and the cello like an inevitable part of my body. The cello, which was once nothing but a filler instrument, used only for continuo ostinato – beautiful phrase: the eternal condition of obstinacy. By Schubert's time the cello starts to be used as a solo instrument (well, actually, that's not entirely correct, Bach used the cello in his cello suites and Marin Marais also composed for the cello, although in truth he was a composer for and a virtuoso of the viola da gamba, a kind of cello, a precursor of the cello). In the Romantic repertoire, the cello was used as a basso continuo in concertos and symphonies, and when

Schubert wrote his Sonata for Arpeggione and Piano, the cello (or in this case the arpeggione) wasn't yet a solo instrument; it took a long time and a lot of hard work for the cello to free itself from its servile role as an instrument of accompaniment, a stubborn continuo. With the Viennese classical period the cello began to be used as a solo instrument in orchestras, just like any other orchestral solo instrument: the violin, the trumpet, the French horn (known as the English horn in Spanish). The cello's dazzling, expressive, extraordinary registers seem to emerge from the soul; the cello is the most human instrument, it can reproduce the sound of a human voice in the precise moment in which a person is experiencing deep pain. And yet, public enthusiasm for the cello didn't have much influence on composers, who continued to write in ways that showcased other instruments, such as the violin: the cello repertoire grew only gradually, so the virtuosos who played most often in salons and concert halls had to pick up their pens and write their own cello compositions or adapt pieces written for other instruments. It would be impossible, now, to dismiss Schubert's Sonata in A minor, D 821, despite the fact it's not really composed for the cello but for the arpeggione, an instrument first made and played in Vienna around 1820, also known back then as a guitar-violoncello or a curved guitar, which, like the true cello, was held between the legs, although its shape and the number of strings – and therefore the sound it produced – were like a guitar. An interesting, hybrid combination – like the voices of the castrati? – an artificial combination that, because of its very nature, was not destined to last. I was and am a cellist, like Jacqueline du Pré, the unfortunate wife of Daniel Barenboim, the pianist I heard play Beethoven's Sonata No. 13 in the Teatro Colón; cellists have to hold the instrument between their legs (as I, Nora García, did and still do, and as Jacqueline du Pré did when she used to play) because when you play the cello it becomes an obstinate part of your own body, until your body is tuned like an instrument. It's a difficult instrument that requires daily practice, because if you don't (as Brailowski used to say, referring to the piano) you'll be the first to notice, to feel it; then your closest friends will warn you (if they too are musicians) and finally, the public. There is no doubt, I repeat, that the body is also an instrument – I know better than anyone, I who have to hold the cello between my legs and mould myself to it, to such a degree that I tend to forget it's an instrument, and it ends up becoming, without my noticing (I reiterate), a mere extension of my own body. And this applies to singers as well as cellists, especially if they sing baroque music – music composed especially for castrati's artificial throats (their larynxes didn't descend because their testicles didn't descend either, as is normal for boys when their voices break, for the pure and simple reason that they had been castrated), yes, in order to play it (baroque music, that is, if you're a singer, a countertenor, or you've been castrated) you have to learn to imitate every instrument, to turn your throat, your whole body into yet another instrument, perhaps one that's less precise, more disturbing and delicate than the instruments made in the eighteenth century, but an instrument that is nonetheless capable of giving the voice flexibility, power, clarity and brightness. Countertenors who are specially trained to take on castrati roles, now that baroque music has become fashionable again, build their voices and then learn to use them as though their existence as instruments were an incontrovertible fact. It's clear that children are more spontaneous, you can tell from their voices when a choir sings a Bach cantata conducted by Nikolaus Harnoncourt. The piano is different, you sit on the stool, legs planted firmly on the ground, or with your toes resting very gently on the pedals (pianists sometimes wear very shiny black shoes or ankle boots, like Daniel Barenboim did in his concerts) and the notes are drawn out, giving them a velvety quality; yes, their hands rest on the keyboard, they lean forward and their faces convey a kind of ecstasy – the ecstasy on the young players' faces in a concert painted by Caravaggio, Michelangelo Merisi – the cello, on the other hand, as I, Nora García, always say, the cello moulds itself entirely to the body, especially women's bodies; female cellists hold the cello between their legs as if it were a man making love to them, that's why in convents novices weren't allowed to touch them, nor were young aristocratic girls, though that's not the case any more, because opening one's legs has become fashionable, and models, even the skeletal ones, are always depicted with their legs open, as though fashion has taken over what was previously consigned to the brothel. The cello has a smaller repertoire and it usually (excepting certain works, such as Bach's cello suites, for instance) has to alternate with other instruments and is only performed in ensemble, in a chamber orchestra, or at the very least accompanied by a piano. Juan played it, he played the piano; I play and played the cello and I don't need nor did I need accompaniment when I play or played pieces for solo cello, for example Bach's cello suites, or Marin Marais's sonatas for viola da gamba. It could be claimed that the piano is more complete than other instruments, that its sonorities are orchestral (although in truth, in orchestral capacity the organ surpasses even the piano, surpasses all other instruments with its vast, tense, sonorous breadth, which was why Bach was primarily an organist, in Leipzig), and this is perhaps immediately noticeable in several of Schubert's piano sonatas. The piano has an advantage over any other instrument because it is self-sufficient, Juan would say, and then would try and prove it, though I didn't, nor do I, agree with him; Juan loved to claim that it didn't need any accompaniment, that that was one of the very reasons why he devoted himself to playing the piano. Yes, Juan played the piano and wrote his compositions on manuscript paper and then, when computers were perfected, he learned to write his compositions directly on a keyboard.

A good musical performance can demonstrate the deepest, most sincere feeling, real feeling, from the heart, feeling that an artist manages to convey in sound, feeling that implies but also surpasses the personal. This is perfectly clear to us: when a piece of music is performed, the voice of the heart is modulated (the universal voice of the heart), because if it weren't, the performance would be inane, entirely empty, sterile and disturbing. That's why most recent performers prefer the instruments and voices for which musical works of the past were originally composed – many of these instruments have obviously disappeared, but there are some that are still perfectly preserved: the oboe da caccia, the regular oboe, the recorder, the transverse flute, the piston trumpet, the bassoon, the cornet, the timpani drum, the horn (the French horn is called the English horn in Spanish), the cello, the viola da gamba, the theorbo, the lute, the violino piccolo. Newer orchestras even use instruments made by seventeenth- and eighteenth-century artisans for a more authentic performance, such as the viola signed by Marcellus Holmayer in Vienna (1650) or Andreas Beer's violoncello piccolo (also in Vienna, in 1685) or Leopold Stastny and Gottfried Hechtl's recorders, signed in 1750 by artisans in Dresden, or, finally, Paulhan's oboe d'amores and oboe da caccias made in 1720, instruments that were used by Nikolaus Harnoncourt's orchestra to play Bach's cantatas alongside child singers in Vienna or

Tölzer or Hanover. It might be impossible, on the other hand, to reproduce the voice of the castrati, something that is best explained by example: the record made at the beginning of the twentieth century that (badly) reproduces the voice of the last castrato sounds guttural and out of tune, like the screaming of a cat in heat. But there is one extraordinary voice, one that perfectly recreates even the most delicate registers of teenagers and women, and it is the voice that emerges from the throat of the countertenor David Daniels (there is also a dwarf singer with a beautiful face whose mother took thalidomide while she was pregnant and whose voice is practically supernatural).

The heart is the centre of life, that human clock, that machine keeping perfect bodily time, a vital flywheel that beats out an arterial concert of tiny signs and so slowly reveals its well-regulated movement. The heart can and should be understood in many different ways, including as a machine governing our physiology, which is to say, as part of a bodily mechanism that keeps us alive and, as such, an object that can be subjected to scientific and technical study. It's important to note that what William Harvey discovered about blood circulation in the seventeenth century was physiological proof of the routes taken by that vital flow, and that Descartes, in his treatise The Passions of the Soul, had already recognised the reciprocal relationship between the heart and the brain: the French philosopher thought that certain passions could produce changes in the blood and express the deepest movements of the heart. Santorio, a Venetian doctor, invented the pulsilogium in 1625, the first machine to calculate cardiac frequency (fifty or a hundred beats per minute), and the Frenchman René Laennec published a study at the beginning of the nineteenth century in which he described the four consecutive steps any good cardiologist should take: examination, auscultation, palpation and percussion. Later, Laennec invented the stethoscope, an instrument that can detect heartbeats and respiratory sounds. Juan would tell us, during the long conversations (monologues, more like) we used to have in this very spot where we're now holding vigil over his body, that the heart was associated with a special symbolism, an ancient devotion to the Sacred Heart of Jesus, a devotion that conferred new meanings on old religious symbols to exalt Christ's corporeality, and thereby his humanity, in a unique way, symbols that account for the coexistence of parallel, mutually influential discourses in science and religion, which also influenced poetry. The heart is the centre of life, that human clock, that machine keeping perfect bodily time, a vital flywheel that slowly reveals, in an arterial concert, its well-regulated movement. Flaubert thought that when women talked about the heart they were really referring to other parts of the body, while Roland Barthes claimed that the word denoted a wide range of movements and desires, which are often given away – though they may be more or less well received, or even rejected. Is the heart the organ of desire? That's how it is conceived, imprisoned, in the imagination (it is of course well known that the heart swells and collapses, like the male member, and also, I would add, that the heart can break, can split in two or three or four, like Juan's). Where will the heart's movements stop? The pure, sincere movements of the heart? I ask myself, now, right here, this very second, with morbid curiosity, what the people attending this funeral are feeling. What do I feel? What could Juan have felt before he died, before his heart shattered into a thousand pieces?

The heart regulates the body, but at the same time it functions – the body – as a kind of shelter or prison for the heart, a prison built to keep out love or the onslaught of destiny: the chest is like a fortress, or rather like protective clothing, to stop feelings from overflowing – the broken heart in your hands. Many poets pulled together an arsenal of war imagery in their poems: the flesh undergoes a metamorphosis and ends up turning into mineral matter to better equip itself against amorous assault – often without success, needless to say. The heart is tempered like steel, and therefore, paradoxically, becomes an object of magnetic attraction: My daughters, Bishop Fernández de Santa Cruz wrote in his will to his favourite nuns, the ones from the Santa Mónica convent in Puebla, my daughters, repeats the bishop, says Juan, reading aloud from the old book, in my last will and testament I command that my heart be removed and buried in your choir, and with you all, so it may lie in death where it lay in life. And so that those who succeed you may remember, set this plaque upon my portrait: Daughters, pray to God for he who gave you his heart. Perhaps I should have asked, before burying him (before burying Juan), for his heart to be delivered to me so I could dissect it and preserve it like a relic, a relic that I could have kept by my bedside, mounted in a heart-shaped frame! (a sublimely cheesy touch) (the most perfect kitsch).

Clare of Montefalco, also called Saint Clare of the Cross, Juan begins again, in another of those long sessions we spent by the unlit fireplace in the other house, sessions during which we all sat listening to him, glasses of tequila in hand (or as I stand by a railing in the garden listening to María's beautiful voice – reminiscent of a castrato – telling the story of his death, Juan's death, the death of the musician who was once my husband), in that living room, I mean, we listened to Juan telling the story of the blessed Clare of Montefalco, who died in the odour of sanctity

84

in 1308 and was subjected to a very special operation, carried out, for the sake of modesty, by the sisters in the convent, who skilfully – suspiciously so (Juan adds in an aside) – chopped up her body and proceeded to remove the guts, handling the heart, which was swollen out of all proportion, with particular care; they immediately put it in a chest before dissecting it the next day in order to ascertain whether the organ's enormous size was a sign of some miracle: when she opened it up one of the nuns found inside, perfectly outlined under the nerves, the shape of the cross made flesh; and when she gently prodded this miraculous heart she discovered another small nerve, also coming away from the organ (the heart, the organ of feeling) and on close examination the nuns found it to be nothing less than the scourge with which Christ had been flagellated; it was (according to the nuns and priests who examined the viscera in order to give their verdict, Juan explained), yes, it was, Juan repeats, it was a replica of the Sacred Heart of Jesus depicted with the instruments of his Passion! Life is an absurd wound.

The Bishop of Santa Cruz's heart, on the other hand, which was protected, while he was still alive, by his pericardial membrane and a wall of ribs, has been described in great detail, almost scientifically, by his contemporaries, those who gave his eulogy (the man with a long, neat moustache who sang the José Alfredo Jiménez song like an opera aria is giving Juan's eulogy in the cemetery chapel), and when we were all talking in the house (our house), even my overbearing, heavyset friend, sitting silently by my side in her austere, navy blue, V-necked jumper, with the glass of tequila in her hand and her heavy shoes on, Juan explains that these analogies of course refer to ancient religious symbolism. The words spoken during the bishop's funeral rites were preserved – forever? – in writing, Juan assures us, and to prove it he read them aloud to us, as though he himself were the prelate in the church in Puebla giving the bishop's eulogy: To teach us how to protect the heart in the life of the spirit, nature herself led the way. She set two guards in the heart, not only to defend it and wall it off for its own protection (Juan is still reading to us in a loud, operatic voice), but also to regulate or delimit its vital movement. The interior membrane, known as the pericardium, is a tunic or sac (like my silk cello case) full of cooling liquid humour that embraces the heart, the space around it adjusting in proportion to its dilation so that nothing, nothing can hurt it, the cooling humour playing an important role; when the membrane is missing, the heart gets tired, damaged, crippled, crippled, which is to say lacerated; and this, ladies and gentlemen, causes a veritable tidal wave of pain.

And Juan would pause for a few moments before reading the rest of the speech in his intense, tragic voice (smoking a cigarette and standing as though to give a eulogy, with more solemnity than the ordinary village priest can muster – the one officiating his own funeral mass, the one standing in front of Juan's coffin in the church inside the convent). Thanks to an abundance of this very humour, the heart is protected, cheered, dilated, drenched in delight. The other guardian of the heart is the chest wall, the fence of the ribs, plus one or two other defences, one or two other guardians whose aim is to protect the origin of life… Nature has raised these walls in order to defend it. In the Bible, King Solomon wants the spiritual, mystical heart – origin and source of the life of the spirit – to be protected by the same guards and defences with which nature herself guards his physical heart. And if these defences are, as I have said, the pericardial membrane and the wall or fence of the ribs, let these two guardians serve in the allegory: in life they are the sepulchre of a living heart, in death the sepulchre of a dead heart.

Jesus's heart, Juan explains, is a blood-making factory, presided over and operated by the eternal father, who uses the heart's blood as though it were fuel, fuel for igniting passion: there is a painting that depicts a garden maintained by a curious hydraulic mechanism, the garden of faith that Christ waters with his own blood.

If nothing but the heart is true, and words are false, how can we make sure our loved one knows – how can they verify – the truth of our passion? The chest is like a breastplate protecting the heart and stopping it from breaking. The mouth seems to express what the heart says, and yet that correlation ends in a rhetorical deception, because words tend to be false. (Juan deceived me, didn't he, although he swore eternal love?) (Perhaps when Rogozhin stabbed Nastasya Filippovna, he was trying to see into the depths of her heart, to reveal her feelings, her real affections.) We have to resort to other bodily organs in order to effect a kind of amorous X-ray of the heart: a displacement occurs: the eyes can substitute the mouth (María's torn mouth, that absurd wound), and can hear as well as see – hear me with your eyes – and, if the loved one cries, the strength of their tears replaces all concepts, becoming irrefutable proof of mute eloquence. María's disappearing mouth? Can a crying person bare their heart? Do tears allow us to glimpse a true heart? Because the broken heart is revealed through tears spilled forth in pain; yes, lovers say: I gave it to you, I gave you my heart, I gave you my heart, my broken heart is in your hands!

His heart broke in their hands, the hands of those who operated on him; Juan is now in the operating room, the surgeons are doing open-heart surgery on him. Hippocrates and Galen imposed a taboo that lasted more than twenty centuries: the heart is sacred:

the heart is situated inside the chest, protected by the pericardium and the ribs, an inner sanctuary, inviolable, inviolable, impossible to penetrate (or to repair): or at least that's what was thought until 1896: on 7 September, the surgeon Jürgen Thorvald recounts, a young gardener called Wilhelm Justus (from the German city of Frankfurt) was stabbed in the heart by three strangers (perhaps they had been drinking themselves into a stupor in the same inn as him) and left for dead in a public park. Three hours later a policeman doing his rounds discovered him at death's door, and took him to the central hospital, where the doctor on call was a young man called Siegel. Justus was unconscious, struggling to breathe, his face sallow, his nostrils quivering, his lips painfully distorted. Siegel observed that he had a stab wound (more than a centimetre wide) near his fourth rib, and examined the kitchen knife responsible, which had been found about a hundred metres from the wounded man. Dr Louis Rehn, a famous surgeon and the hospital's chief physician, wouldn't be back until the next day. Siegel observed that the knife had penetrated the heart, which was still beating, although the pulse was very weak; he took a probe and inserted it carefully to calculate the damage, which was evidently considerable. Siegel was certain Justus would die at any moment; his heartbeat was faint, fifty beats per minute. The policeman who had brought him in hadn't left his side and asked if there was any chance of survival. Siegel shook his head, remembering as he did so what one of the most renowned surgeons in Germany had once said: any surgeon who dares penetrate the heart will surely lose forever the respect of his colleagues. Siegel was not an exceptional doctor, but he did understand that, although the wound was small, an internal haemorrhage was slowly but surely killing the patient, draining him of blood; he also undoubtedly remembered that Hippocrates and Galen had pronounced, several centuries ago, that wounds to the heart would cause inevitable death.

Siegel gave orders for the patient to receive camphor and for the wound to be iced. The policeman still hadn't moved, and eventually asked (somewhat hesitantly) if Dr Rehn would be back soon. Siegel was offended: did he doubt his skill as a doctor? He knew the patient would be dead by the time Rehn came into the surgery the next day.

But he was not.

Rehn examined Justus: his face was marked by death by now, practically bloodless, his pulse distant and weak, his wrist damp with sweat, his breathing shallow, his lungs severely compromised by the internal haemorrhage; but the external wound wasn't bleeding any more, just throbbing weakly. Rehn quickly took stock of the situation: the knife had penetrated the pericardium, touching (or perhaps barely scratching) the wall with its tip, but any wound of that type would produce a slow drip and blood would gradually invade the heart until it prevented it from beating by increasing the pressure implacably, as was the case with Nastasya Filippovna. Perhaps the wound was serious enough to allow blood to leak into the thoracic cavity (the thoracic cavity broadens in a very particular way in young, castrated men, such that their vocal range expands and they are able to reach very intense registers). Yes, Rehn said to himself, the heart has not been fatally compressed, so Justus has a very slim chance of survival. The heart will continue working until it squeezes out the last drop of blood, then the blood will invade the lungs and put such pressure on them that the patient will stop breathing (did something similar happen to

Nastasya Filippovna?). I'm going to try something, he said to himself – if I don't then this is a death sentence anyway. Did he think, before doing it, about some of the previous attempts to penetrate that (theretofore) inviolable sanctuary? The case of a man in the era of Napoleon who attempted suicide by stabbing himself in the heart, and who the famous surgeon Larrey tried (fruitlessly) to save by opening the patient's chest (with no anaesthetic) and touching for the first time with his finger (the middle one), the tip of a heart?! Or the case of an English tinker who (in 1872) was (successfully) operated on by an English surgeon named Callender, who pulled a needle, with which the tinker had been stabbed during an altercation in a brothel, out of his heart? Didn't Callender make a miniscule incision in the chest to retrieve the needle, which was sinking and re-emerging according to the rhythmic movements of the systole and diastole?

But never before had there been a case of a surgeon daring to open up a patient's chest entirely in order to rummage around inside their heart. He must have felt a shiver down his spine, a sudden wave of nausea – did his blood pressure rise and his pulse accelerate (a hundred and fifty or two hundred beats per minute?): what did it feel like to open a chest, to violate it, to penetrate the sanctuary for the first time and then have – finally! – a (broken) heart in his hands? To expose it completely, to contemplate its workings, to make an incision (or two incisions), to staunch the bleeding, insert a needle, sew, tack, suture, close the chest again, wait until the sternum is soldered? How do you take a beating heart in your hands (human sacrifice?), how do you insert a needle into a muscle that is ceaselessly moving? how do you work with its well-regulated movement? its arterial concert? But it wasn't enough just to imagine, he had to decide, decide to break into the prison, to take the (broken) heart in his hands.

Justus was still alive, very weak now, but he withstood the anaesthesia. Rehn made a broad incision in the sternum – so difficult to penetrate the bone! (splinters flying) – and once he had he could hear the weak beating of the heart much more clearly; he made a new incision near the fifth rib – the thorax was full of clotted blood – stuck one of his fingers (the middle one?) in and felt the pericardium. He then cut through the pleura and there was a lot more blood (his assistants could barely contain it) and the lung collapsed. Would the heart cope? The pericardium appeared and the damage the knife had done to the muscle was visible. He tried to secure it with some tweezers so he could work, to open the incision a little more and penetrate still deeper. Several times he had to repeat the operation because the pericardial membrane kept tearing and blood would gush out. He finally managed to move the pericardium to one side and to reach the heart: there it was, beating irregularly in its continual movement of expansion (diastole) and contraction (systole); he could see what kind of wound the knife had made, right in the middle of the right ventricle; it measured about a centimetre long and blood was seeping gently out. Instinctively, Rehn put his finger on it: the wound immediately stopped bleeding. His finger slipped every time the heart contracted, but when it expanded he could feel the wound again; he tried closing it with a fine needle and silk thread, taking advantage of the constant alternating expansion and contraction that keeps the heart alive. He made use of the diastole, when the wound was exposed. In one agile movement he made the first stitch on the left side, then waited a moment (a century more like) for the heart to resume its rhythm before he made the second stitch, fearing constantly that the heart would stop beating. When he finished suturing, the wound stopped bleeding and the pulse became firmer. He cleaned the pericardium and the thorax of clotted blood, put the rib back in its place and closed the external wound. Two hours later, Justus was breathing easily.

If you're not careful, on arrival in the city of La Paz, Bolivia you might die of a sudden heart attack. In order to avoid this, you should take it easy for three days during which your red blood cell count will increase and your blood will become oxygenated again, before returning to life at a normal pace. A famous German orchestra director died immediately after disembarking at Los Altos airport, which is about four thousand metres above sea level: a sudden heart attack put an end to a long and successful career.

If I'm not mistaken, it wasn't until 1948 that surgeons once again dared open a patient's chest and dilate one of their valves. Open-heart surgery was to become routine within ten years and, from 1970 onwards, scientific progress in that area was staggering. The patient must be placed temporarily in a non-physiological situation because the organism cannot withstand circulation being halted for longer than three minutes. In the past, different procedures were used to achieve this, such as hypothermia (body temperature would reach twenty-eight degrees centigrade) and hyperbaria, which involves increasing the concentration of oxygen in the blood. These days, they use artificial organs, a heart and a lung, to maintain blood supply to the brain.

The cleanness of language used to write sentimental poetry, poetry that talks of the heart, reflects the quality of the tears – their transparency; what's more, long before open-heart surgery existed it was possible to destroy that impenetrable shield holding the inner organ inside the thorax, covered by muscles and skin, through the simple strength of love, which operates by way of alchemical transmutation to produce amorous precipitation, that liquid humour, which, the result of extreme passion, is irrefutable – if metaphorical – proof of a faithful and loving heart, broken by passion (and the love of truth). To operate on Juan, the doctors wear fine latex gloves and their instruments are stained with blood, a much thicker humour than tears, which are transparent. Tears allow the lover to show the transition between the invisible and the visible: feelings that seem disingenuous when expressed with mere words and concrete actions – for example with physical affection or gifts – are pale reflections of their truth, the heart's truth; the only sincere and beautiful thing are the tears that moisten the lovers' hands, like the tears that once spilled from my eyes onto Juan's hands as he held my face, tears that were irrefutable proof of my truest, most profound feelings. Can the vulgar heating of the blood, an alchemical reaction, reaffirm the miracle of requited love?

Certain changes to the blood provoke movements in the face, such as joy or despair: the blood warms, thins, convulses – can blood convulse? or is it the heart that convulses? Yes, amorous passion puts physiological mechanisms in motion; yes, under the influence of passion the blood warms and produces a kind of effervescence that pushes it out of the heart, yes, that open wound that is life. And that's literally what happens when you're unlucky in love: the fire of love makes the heart, the organ of life, break – my broken heart is in your hands; those strong feelings allow the blood to boil, it's true, it's completely true, the blood boils and combustion takes place, just like when you put a pot on to boil and the water evaporates, the heating process creates a poetic movement: the transmutation of words into tears distils and vaporises the blood in a stinging of the eyes. According to the amorous metaphor, the heart is apparently distilled like liquor, although in reality – assuming you're alive – the chest still has its shield and tears are just the expression – a copy – of requited passion. There is one unique formula for breaking a heart, metaphorically breaking it into pieces through passion, or turning it into a transparent liquid that will serve as a mirror. We might describe this possibility by saying that certain ways of dying turn death into a liquid, which is to say, they turn it into duration and purification. To ensure a heart will break, not metaphorically but literally, you need open-heart surgery, so that the chest spurts blood and extinguishes the lascivious flame. When the thorax is truly pierced, when that strongbox guarding the chest – made up of the sternum and the ribs – is broken, when the chest is split violently open, death comes suddenly, just as Juan's death came suddenly, or the death of Nastasya Filippovna, who perhaps could have been saved if they'd performed open-heart surgery on her, as a German surgeon named Rehn performed on a patient in 1896.

In her convulsive speech, María has said the word death, Juan's death, and blood seems to spurt from her mouth, disrupting nature, staining it red. Death is perhaps the most violent form of romantic connection, if blood flows from the two chests, bound together. It's Juan's blood that's been spilt. I hear my own rhythmic pulse, my blood, steady, steady as a metronome (between fifty and a hundred beats per minute), inside my own heart, as I monitor it. Thus the two chains of metaphors are resolved, that of the heart and tears, and that of the heart and blood, two means of producing liquid, two means of breaking a heart, the only two means of destroying the prison, that fence of bones and flesh. In murder, in suicide (if in the murder or suicide in question the chest has been violently pierced and the heart exposed) or in an operation (to replace the body's arteries with plastic ones or to repair the tissues of the mitral valve using a valve from a pig or a cow) the chest is split open and the heart comes into view; what's more, the doctors can take it in their hands – Juan's broken heart in their hands. Yes, says Sor Juana, because I, wiser in my fortune, have both my eyes in my hands and see only what I touch.

Olive oil, María explains, interrupting her tale (mouth gleaming), contains 77% monounsaturated fats, good fats (HDL), the ones that help reduce bad cholesterol (LDL). Researchers believe that olive oil – María repeats, her mouth meagre, her lips pressed bitterly together – can reduce the risk of heart disease and some types of cancer; plus, it helps regulate blood pressure and alleviate arthritis. Easily digestible, she adds, olive oil can reduce gastric acid, heal ulcers, and stimulate liver, intestine and pancreas function (as perhaps can avocado). If you don't have high blood pressure, she adds, you don't have to worry too much, even if your cholesterol is high, at our age cholesterol doesn't mean anything any more; that said, she says, raising her voice even more (making everyone around us turn to listen), you must avoid increasing your blood pressure (but I know that what she's saying isn't true: cholesterol really is bad, to counteract it you have to watch your diet and take Lipitor or Zokor or Mevacor although they damage the liver (and to prevent hepatic complications you must have regular check-ups, at least once every six months)).

As for me, I allow myself to sketch a poetic fantasy, to trace a relationship between the heart, that indispensable organ that draws a hieroglyph of our feelings – the physiology of love? – and the sonnet form. Like the heart, the sonnet closes in on itself; it can never leave its frame, even when the vapours of passion start brimming in the eyes. I believe that, as an effect of combustion – which is nothing more than a thermal combination – the heart can dissolve into tears, break, destroy itself. The sonnet form is very similar to that of the heart, that delicate instrument, closed in on itself, which when it overflows causes the body – in this particular case, Juan's body – as well as the poem, to die.

Beginning and end meet, as in the esoteric symbol of the ouroboros, the snake that bites its own tail (perfect allegory of the infinite and also of eternal return) (we might say wrestling with the angel). The cobblestone village is beautiful, nestled in the mountains, a slender blue colour, the streets rising and falling towards the dusty plaza. Nothing seems to have changed since the last time I was here; Juan's death is the only thing that changes anything, like his house that's changed, our house; perhaps it rains less these days because the earth is noticeably grey in colour – like the grey of his face and of the rough texture of the moustache that disfigures him, perhaps. I've seen stacks of dry hay piled up stubbornly in the fields, packed clumsily, tousle-haired, po-faced, hungry- and thirsty-looking, left haphazardly to weather the elements, not like in those still lifes Juan and I admired in European museums, those Dutch and Spanish paintings, the Spanish ones with their fruit and insects, the Dutch ones with their bright fields, the sun shining on dozens of haystacks, illuminating them from within; bundles of hay that will feed the animals and fill the grain stores, gathered and packed by the farmers, the yellow hay of the fields piled up to form perfectly triangular, perfectly balanced pyramids, painted with great technical expertise and a delicate spirit, stacks and stacks of hay crowned with knots, a final touch in the silence, the silence of an autumnal peace. In other paintings the farmers sit and eat in groups, children play, men drink, other men slice bread, a woman tucks her hair into her headdress; behind her, the piles of hay are triumphant structures whose stubborn presence contributes to the sense of abundance; you examine the painting from one end to another, making an inventory of the objects that appear there, and for me what stands out most is the passive, sweet surrender of the bright bundles of yellowing hay, that autumnal peace Gould hoped to achieve when he played, shortly before he died, the Goldberg Variations by Johann Sebastian Bach.

On Mexico's roads, as I'm driving to the village to add myself to the list of mourners – parishioners – at a wake, the haystacks fill me with melancholy, in their worn, untidy appearance, the fragile shadow of a loss, I think, when I cross the village's main street (which also serves to connect the surrounding villages) with its improvised vegetable stalls, piled up sacks of carrots, ribbons of meat, orange and green chorizos, flies buzzing, the church bells tolling sadly in my heart. In the Dutch paintings, industriousness is rewarded by a strip of green suggesting fertile land, almost idyllic in its glorification of everyday values, the hay a reminder of an abundant harvest where there is a use for every smug, efficient piece of straw.

I'm still standing near the coffin, staring almost unblinkingly at the sallow face with that new, unfortunate moustache occupying the space where the teeth should be, a straw-coloured face with the jaw strapped up so it doesn't fall away, an anonymous, unseeing face. When someone is mythified – is memory at fault? – a story is created and new and fleeting bodies are engendered; words always correct those bodies, transform them, polishing their faces, Juan's face, the face I remember Juan having, the Juan I spent many years with, whose deathly face reminds me of the colour of haystacks in the fields (the happy fields in my memory and the ones in the Dutch paintings we contemplated together in those early days when we still held each other's hands), it's becoming the face of someone the years have not been kind to, an incessant movement seems to be etching every line, the remains of the model are dissolving, new features are being sketched – will they substitute the ones I remember? will this face I'm seeing now, for the last time, be his definitive face?

It's not him any more, I'm not me any more, we are no longer, we are others, as though we wanted to escape ourselves, behind our own backs, through our eyes, through our stomachs, through our chests, I look curiously at him again, remembering his outpourings of affection, all that time ago, and ask myself, as I did then: how far does he want to go? Or rather, how far did he want to go? Outpourings of affection that wrenched you from your own body one organ at a time, one fragment at a time, unfolding it, multiplying it; I remember that curiosity would keep me (sometimes, not always) on the alert, and that a desperation to know meant I couldn't completely enjoy anything; I wanted to know, I always wanted to know how far we would go, it clouded everything, and then pleasure itself, total pleasure, which was sometimes followed by nausea or disgust – or are they the same thing? – immense disgust, rejection, no more hugs or kisses or sighs or promises, a few tears, thick like sperm, gentle, deft affection, tender but also sticky, asphyxiating – sordid? A heart tainted by its own corrupt projects, a heart aching from so much misery.

Is that what the burial is going to be like? I ask myself, interrupting the memory, my body stabilising, the nausea easing: light, tender, deft but also sticky, asphyxiating, sordid? How do you describe sordidness? Can I explain it just by repeating the word sordidness? Everything is jumbled, sordidness, tenderness, but at the same time the parodic, the flies, shit, pebbles, huaraches, dirty feet, each leg like a hoof, the drunk beggar with a bandaged foot, the bandage stained with fresh blood, the route marked by the tracks of oxen and cows, of horses' hooves. Effort is painted on the beggar's face, every step painful – the hill must be climbed, there is dust, pebbles, cowpats – his gait is pitiful and at the same time obscene; his impertinent gaze develops into a crude expression that accompanies the corpse, the corpse of a diminished man, nothing more than dried out, sallow skin, the colour of the haystacks speckling the landscape all the way along the main road, poorly-tied, tousle-haired, measly bundles, their worn appearance in keeping with a landscape that itself is worn down by drought, by uncontrolled logging, the earth a sterile, sickly yellow. A man whose heart used to beat regularly (fifty or a hundred beats per minute) but which has stopped: a heart wounded by death. Will someone finally announce that it is to me, Nora García, that condolences should be offered?

I take the subway, the red line, towards the Museum of Fine Art in Boston. Opposite me is an advertisement: Do you take insulin for diabetes? Keep an eye on your heart. Mine, naturally, is beating quickly, more than a hundred beats per minute. The ticket costs twelve dollars, because I'm a pensioner; if I were a normal person, it would have cost me sixteen: I console myself with the knowledge that I can come back to the museum as many times as I want until the end of the month. It's a vast museum, very modern, full of US flags, big flags, little flags, and flying through the air are multicoloured statues, young, healthy, flexible athletes with perfectly healthy hearts. I move through numerous galleries full of installations and paintings, almost without pausing, stopping only at certain frames, certain statues, certain photographs (which they almost always exhibit in the hallways, as though they're not sure which category they fall into: art or document). I enter a dimly lit room where I find the last Japanese temple to be built in the eighth century, Anno Domini, brought over whole from Japan by some illustrious Bostonians who decided to buy it before it was torn down; it's an oratory reserved for priests, without a flock now, with a group of curious onlookers instead who are carefully observing the wood-panelled walls, the lamps, the buddhas.

The room next door houses miniatures, jade perfume bottles with coral stoppers or cinnabar ones with aventurine stoppers (or marble with amethyst); I examine them carefully, get bored, walk around other rooms that are equally enormous, a succession of glass cases full of amphorae, hydriai, Greek kraters, Egyptian sarcophagi, necklaces and combs and boxes and cats and enormous, ramrod-stiff statues with elaborate, impossible hairstyles, always with their right foot forward, all perfectly conserved as though they were made yesterday, objects identical to the ones in the Metropolitan Museum in New York, in the Louvre, in the British Museum, and in the Pergamon in Berlin, as though the lands of Egypt or Greece or Rome or Mexico did nothing but produce thousands and thousands of little figures, vessels, tombs and statues that would end up decorating museums the world over and still have enough material left to grace the less elegant, less well-organised museums in their countries of origin. Thank goodness, I think, thank goodness millionaires are so obsessed with collecting a specific type of object and keeping them in their palaces, and then, when they die, bequeathing them to museums so their galleries will flaunt plaques with their names on, like tombstones. Personally, I prefer Lila Acheson's approach: the enormous niches where you can find immense flower arrangements in the foyer of the Met are a perpetual tribute to her memory.

A connection occurs to me as I walk through the vast galleries of the huge Marshall Fields shopping centre in Chicago (situated on the Magnificent Mile), a multistorey building inside which the first floor is always visible: there, all manner of objects are carefully arranged: dresses by famous designers, jumpers, raincoats, towels, pots and pans, cosmetics, children's clothes, swimsuits, rugs, objects displayed elegantly to attract consumers. The day I visited, there was no one there, I was completely alone; the place had the same quiet, funereal air (as in an old-fashioned funeral or a gringo graveyard, ascetic and aseptic) as those huge museum galleries housing permanent collections you have to pass through on your way to the temporary exhibitions, which by contrast are full of people because they've only just opened, only just been announced and reviewed in the papers and magazines, the deeper signifi- cance of which you'll understand better if you rent a pair of headphones with recordings in all the major languages, and then eventually, when you leave the exhibition, you can buy yourself a souvenir, an imitation gemstone, a postcard, a card, a catalogue, a necklace, a bag, a handker- chief, a tie, a jumper.

There's a news item on the radio and in the papers: in a crematorium in the state of Georgia bodies abandoned more than twenty years ago have been found, some of them still decomposing: their relatives had received standard issue urns full of nothing but lime and earth. Abuse, violence, and even rape are being denounced in old people's homes. Jesuit priests are still sexually abusing children in their parishes. It won't be long before we return to the use of atomic bombs to combat evil.

For some reason I can't quite explain, as I write these lines describing Juan's funeral, I'm reading Sebald or Dostoyevsky, Bernhard or Rousseau, listening to Seppi Kronwitter, the young Tölzer singer in the recording of Bach's cantata (who, thanks to this recording, will forever be a child, or rather, his voice will forever be preserved in its perfect, angelic childhood state, through the magic art of recording), conducted by Nikolaus Harnoncourt; certain characters are seated: he is, they are, I am too. After we separated, Juan lived for a while in a modest house in the village and got himself around on an old bicycle. But in my text, he's listening as he writes, as I am, to Rameau's Pygmalion. He's listening to it as he writes in his diary or notates music on his manuscript paper (crucial work that allowed Jean-Jacques Rousseau to earn a living) and it's playing on a simple radio cassette player; I'm listening on a traditional record player and I'm sitting in my red chair writing on a typewriter. The table is large, rough, greenish from use and from cooking acids – olive oil – that have stained it forever (or for the rest of its existence): In this precise moment the record scratches (I would have liked to have Juan's cassette player, especially because mine plays acetate discs, totally archaic now that we're in the age of the DVD) and the countertenor's ambiguous voice repeats l'amour, l'amour, l'amour endlessly, words that I too repeat, and that Juan repeats in his choral works and with exemplary consistency in his diaries. Juan writes his papers and I write mine. And in this way, the two of us sit conversing. Him in the photograph, me in my house, sitting at the table on a black velvet cushion – world record for tackiness – with its crochet fringing that goes with the malignant red of the chair; next to it, pleonastic, bright, soft, the red silk pin cushion (like a tango? or a chocolate filled with cherry liqueur?).

Juan is unhappy, or at least that's what I would like to believe. One day he left his wife (me, Nora García) and children and started a chaotic, greedy life, but it doesn't matter now, in my text he's sitting at a table writing in his diary in his perfect handwriting, with his gold pen (also obsolete, like the act of writing by hand) – he's writing something but I can only make out a phrase or two. Pygmalion is singing or reciting impassioned words, he's in love, he's madly in love, the way people only ever love each other in novels or operas, his voice (sometimes patient, sometimes stumbling) accompanying the delicate scratching of a pen leaving indelible marks in a white notebook. Juan has lived a debauched life (what do I mean by that?) but now he's writing (as I wish, jealously, that I were) and his writing reduces him to a strange passivity, sitting monotonously at a table (Rogozhin waits, sitting patiently by Nastasya Filippovna's body, with the four unstoppered bottles of Zhdanov disinfectant instead of altar candles, until Prince Myshkin arrives), taking a pen (some people prefer pencils), placing it between his thumb, index and middle finger, and putting the tips of his fingers, placing the tips of his fingers on the keys of a Remington typewriter, or an Olympia, or an electric one that's even faster (why would it be faster, whether it's a normal typewriter or an electric one or a computer, if it follows the pace of your writing? Only handwriting is slower – yes, that much is true). We write as though we're writing something we actually lived (Casanova is the best example, he wrote letters to his patrons and love letters to his lovers, and he wrote his memoirs when life – that absurd wound – stopped him from living as he wanted to, once he was old and infirm – his body totally ruined before he even turned sixty – those years, the last years of his life, I mean, when he was writing his memoirs, while he worked as a librarian at a castle in Bohemia that belonged to the Count of Dux). Or perhaps life is divided and one way of living is to fulfil that strange desire to stay still, like Juan now, lying in his casket, and me staring at him as I sit next to the coffin? Or perhaps he's somewhere else, sitting on a black velvet cushion with crocheted fringing, at an old, rough, country kitchen table (whose smoothness and age is broken by an absurd, heart-shaped, red silk pin cushion). (I close my eyes: I can see him now, stretched out, practically naked before me on a table, his body perforated by needles, in his chest, in his stomach, in his ears, above his eyebrows, his world-weary forehead, even in the skin of his neck near the jugular, an intense wound, the absurd wound that is life: it's all so fleeting! Your heart is made of glass!) When I write, my hands move in a very different way to Juan's hands when he plays the piano or mine when I play the cello, because I played and still play the cello; essentially, in order to make music on the cello and other string instruments, you take the bow and place it over the bridge and your right hand moves wisely and delicately in order to produce a deep, melancholy sound, like a lament, especially audible when Jacqueline du Pré, already sick, presses the strings with her index and middle fingers so her instrument produces the highest, most moving, though by now slightly imperfect, sounds. Here, on the other hand, I'm writing on a typewriter and the tapping of my fingers on the machine is monotonous, mediocre, bureaucratic, very different from the powerful sound produced by string instruments. An extraordinary passivity obliges us to stop living in order to write, thinking that that is life. On the record, Pygmalion sounds proud – we know this because the sumptuousness of his voice is coupled with the trumpets' bright, metallic tones, a sharp sound that vibrates in the closed space of the theatre or soars in the open air with the call to the hunt (in Telemann's sonatas for trumpet, for example), a sound that can be heard in the recording once made of a group of musicians playing with sincerity, with specificity – like María's voice, perhaps, when I bump into her in the garden and she starts to tell me again the details of Juan's death, while her lipsticked mouth disappears, leaving barely the sketch of lips lined in a darker colour, pressed bitterly together, or perhaps reminiscent of a heart-shaped, red silk pin cushion that I have on the table?

And all the devotion and all the sorrows and all the bodies and all the pleasures are concentrated in this hand running swiftly across the page which is gradually filling up with perfect characters (Arial font, size 14, Hewlett Packard, gold Mont Blanc pen, broad nib), an attempt to halt life, to preserve the memory of life (l'amour, Pygmalion sings, l'amour toujours, and María insists: his heart was broken), the dark wound that is life. I can hear Rameau as I sit here, that same countertenor (a photograph of David Daniels: wide, pear-shaped face, hair – a lot of it – falling over his forehead, highlighting his thick eyebrows and thin moustache, more like a bit of fluff covering his upper lip, his chin and jaw also covered by a fledgling beard), that same countertenor, I repeat, David Daniels, is singing a melancholy aria (it's no longer Rameau, it's Handel, but the voice of a well-trained falsetto singing soprano rings passionately, singing of sadness, disillusionment, abandonment), he sings like the castrati used to sing: the lightness, flexibility and higher pitch of his voice set it apart from male voices, its brightness, purity and power set it apart from women's voices, and its perfect adult musculature, technique and expressivity make it superior to children's voices, and as a result of all that, those high-pitched sounds resemble a soprano or the child singers on the recording of one of Bach's cantata's (the voice of young Seppi Kronwitter, conducted by Nikolaus Harnoncourt), because the anguished modulations of countertenors are interrupted suddenly when they slip into male falsetto. One day I discovered a voice that tore at my heart: Seppi's voice, the voice of the child Seppi Kronwitter. I discovered him one day while listening to the cantatas recorded by Nikolaus Harnoncourt and Gustav Leonhardt, and in one of them he is leading the young Tölzer singers. The first time I heard that voice my pulse quickened, as it were – my heart broke. The passage that gets me is only a few minutes long, perhaps just two, before another of the soloists from the choir replaces him, Peter Jelosits; he sings much better, more in tune, his voice fuller, more like a professional soprano, but Seppi's voice trembles like a bird you've cupped in your hands to rescue it from some enclosed space it entered by mistake (as often happens in my greenhouse), he runs out of breath and when he tries to reach the highest registers his voice breaks and then suddenly, as quickly as it arrived, disappears, I rewind the CD and repeat the passage that so excited me (a true orgasm of the soul) (several times), but his voice has become like any other, a wonderful, well-pitched voice, nothing more than that. I try again (it's useless), then I don't listen to the cantatas for a long time, several months go by, I've forgotten which cantata it is, and I'm thrilled by the beauty of those I listen to, the composer's extraordinary skill and the adequate (coherent) performance of the piece (and of course, the enormous majesty of Bach's music). I continue my detective work, which doesn't involve finding a perfect voice but rather re-finding the voice that in the past has moved me, a voice I've come across on a couple of records, a voice I've lost and which I am still stubbornly seeking. I work systematically, listening (on the CD player) one by one, in ascending order, to Bach's cantatas played by Harnoncourt or Gustav Leonhardt, and when finally I arrive at Cantata No. 52 the miracle occurs again: I hear the voice, Seppi Kronwitter's voice, a voice somewhere between childhood and adolescence, a natural voice that only lasts an instant, the instant a boy stops being a boy and begins his mature years, that crucial moment in which his larynx and testicles descend at the same time. It's an ephemeral voice, sharp, transparent, unstable (unless you operate on boys when they're six or seven so the larynx retains the position, shape and plasticity of infancy) (the castrati grew disproportionately tall and were a beautiful mixture of man-boy-woman that made them irresistible, they awoke perverse desires among audience members, although in order to ward off those feelings some people insulted or made fun of them): Seppi's voice is (or was) natural, an adolescent voice, an intermediary voice, before the break, because adolescent voices break.

I'm at the cinema watching a silent film (is it Metropolis by Fritz Lang?), Juan puts his arm around my shoulders (I'm eating chocolate-covered raisins and he's eating popcorn), a man is playing the piano. It's Satie's Three Pieces in the Shape of a Pear, which Juan also plays in the living room on the Bösendorfer, better suited for playing Schubert than the Steinway or the Petrof. No, it's not Satie any more, it's Handel again, adapted for piano. Daniels is suffering and his voice evokes Cleopatra, the only woman he has ever loved, and the actor (another countertenor), as protean as any good actor, sings a sacred song and life becomes eternal, thanks to a sense of calm and to undulating music (a Solomonic column). That's how I, Nora García, sitting at the typewriter (or in front

of the computer) in a wide, grey skirt or opening my
black trouser-clad legs as I play the cello, while he, Juan,
immobile in the memory, writes non-stop in his diary
using his Mont Blanc pen (it's manuscript paper, he's in
his (modest) house in the countryside, before he moved
here, where we're now holding vigil over him in the
immense studio where there's a piano (a Bösendorfer, a
Steinway, or a Petrof?) and several other musical instruments: a cello, flutes, violins (Amati, Stradivarius), sheet
music, books, paintings, flowers, altar candles) (and a
lingering, cloying smell of clotted blood); he has shut
himself away for a while to write his books (the culmination of his research) in peace, and his compositions
for piano (he notates directly onto staves on manuscript
paper – computers don't exist yet) and thus this space
and that time are preserved, the time I spent talking to
him as we sat at my green kitchen table that still bears
the trace of various substances (primitive alchemy) (my
desk where a red silk pin cushion lies useless, five needles
piercing it like the therapeutic needles that pierced Juan's
body) and I tapped the typewriter keys with the tips of
my fingers and listened to Rameau's Pygmalion sung by
David Daniels and he, Juan, with this thick, gold (Mont
Blanc) pen narrated his life by writing in his diaries in
an ink that reminds me of the colour of the Emmanuelle
Khanh suit María is wearing this very moment, that
brilliant, diabolical, heavily perfumed woman who, as she
accompanies me on the rocky walk to the cemetery, talks
tirelessly, despite the ascent, of Juan's death: that's life, she
repeats, that's life, bitch, as your mum used to say, life's
a bitch every single day, you know only too well, life is
an absurd wound. And she adds, in her gramophone-like
voice: these days women don't need men to surround
them with luxury, nor do men need women to conceal
their homosexuality. That's what tango is: an ordering

principle of pleasure and, at the same time, a discourse, more nostalgic than melancholic, more visceral than narcissistic. You don't need anybody in order to suffer. The melancholic – and only bad tango composers are melancholy – swallows everybody else and spits out the bones.

Bach's Cantata 52, conducted by Nikolaus Harnoncourt, is performed by a choir, an orchestra and a soloist (a soprano), in this case the child Seppi Kronwitter. Bach composed it on 24 November 1726, a year during which he was still writing a cantata a week. The text refers to the Gospel. The work's structure is surprisingly simple and clear: the perfidy of the world and the goodness of God are expressed in a recitative and an aria respectively, and the whole thing is introduced by an instrumental symphony. The cantata concludes with a choral verse in F major, though the reference key is D minor. The perfidious world is expressed in F major and the kingdom of heaven in B flat. The melody is simple, despite the over-the-top instrumentation, perhaps because it uses, as in a symphony, the first movement of the first Brandenburg Concerto (without the piccolo). The bright sounds of the sinfonia concertante contrast with the sonic asceticism of the first air (with its two violins and the basso continuo played on the harpsichord). A true Christian rejects the false world and scorns it with imprecations, says the priest at Juan's funeral. The sweetness of the aria, titled God is Faithful, repeated several times, is a counterpoint to the hostile rejection in the first recitative. The second air is illuminated by the continuous sound of three oboes; their dancing character (it's almost a polonaise) praises the glory of the divine world and the dance of the soul, which is the dance of the true Christian. When the choir verse ends, the whole orchestra takes up the theme again, marked by the first horn which reinforces the young soprano's heartrending song, sung by Seppi Kronwitter, who in this recording (made in 1970) was fifteen years old and who is now (perhaps) forty-seven. His child's voice was unique, metallic, nasal and fragile, very slender, almost transparent; the young singer Peter Jelosits (another young soprano) who accompanies Cantata 58, also conducted by Harnoncourt, has a voice that is fuller, more tuneful, more professional, but Seppi's, tender and modulated, is moving, it breaks like a bird flapping against the windows of the living room of this huge house. The only genuine performances of Bach's cantatas are those that include young choral singers, Harnoncourt believes, following Bach, who composed for the boys in the choir he himself directed in St Thomas's Church in Leipzig, a choir his own sons, Philip Emmanuel and Johann Christian, joined when they were teenagers. Harnoncourt prefers to use young singers and original, contemporary instruments to give authenticity to his performances, although you can (also) hear in his recordings the voices of several famous countertenors, sopranos, basses and baritones (as I said, Juan reiterates, the last time Gould played the Goldberg Variations was in a broadcast titled by the pianist himself: To Each His Own Bach).

As I walk beside the beggar, I can see his fresh blood (Juan's has stopped flowing); inside the coffin the body is wearing the same clothes, the ones they've dressed him in for the last time, casual, outdoor clothes, banal, really – English-looking? well-to-do English country clothes? – whose dried-out, melancholy colour is thrown into relief by the sad tie and black handkerchief protecting his toothless jaw. I can see the beggar's fresh blood, it's staining the bandages on his injured foot as he walks the dusty path in his dusty huaraches. That damp smell is still dogging me, climbing with me, accompanying me. The imposing fat man, the one with a voice like a trombone (his name is Eduardo), the one beside the thin, well-dressed woman wearing not a shred of make-up who smiles mechanically as he spouts his pompous nonsense, Eduardo, yes, Eduardo asks if he too can share the weight of the coffin, he asks just as it's changing hands, when the people who have been carrying it up till now are to be swapped out, the men I mean, it's always men, the men who have been carrying it along the rocky path that dips and climbs all the way to the cemetery, a path surrounded by mountains – it's right at that moment that Eduardo goes over, leaving the thin woman behind (who could she be? his new wife?), he goes over, bends forward and places the coffin on his shoulders in a single, essential movement, ensuring it stays in the air. Impossible: Eduardo is so immense, so different in height to the other men that the coffin is no longer supported properly, the weight cannot be equally shared, the coffin wobbles: Eduardo pants, goes red, sweats. A humble-looking man in shirtsleeves, dusty shoes and a very battered pair of trousers quickly goes over, takes Eduardo's place, sits the rough-hewn, white pine wood coffin with its gold rivets onto his shoulder, and the cortège continues along the path, rising and falling, littered with cowpats, dust, and pebbles.

The path is long, very long, and the coffin rocks like a cradle on the men's shoulders, over the stones and pebbles, with mariachi songs, mezcal, tequila, dirty toes poking out of holey shoes. I'm wearing boots covered in dust. My new haircut makes me look younger, María's too, she's walking beside me. They walk, we all walk, as though in procession, we've got all the elements of one: children crying and licking their snotty noses, housekeepers in their black Sunday best, campesinos with hard, gaunt faces, serious and proud, wearing

parched-looking sombreros to keep the sun off, local
officials in colourful shirts, jeans, coarse cloth trousers,
with moustaches as wispy as their skin, bony hands and
stiff, heavy, short-brimmed hats, the orchestra directors,
the official with his ceremonial outfit and a thick (very
smooth, neat) moustache, the one who sang that José
Alfredo Jiménez song with the mariachis as though it
were an opera aria, the rich ladies who spend weekends
in their comfortable, luxurious country homes, who
play their grand pianos while Juan, glass in hand, keeps
the beat, women whose designer shoes are also covered
in dust as they walk near the mariachis with their faded
suits and worn-out, raspy voices, near the violinists and
the pianists who aren't crying because it wouldn't be
manly, the dwarf flautist, the starving, yellow-eyed street
dogs, the orchestra conductors in their dark grey and
white pinstriped suits or navy blue, gold-buttoned, fine
cashmere blazers, the black cat running across the path
(the ladies cross themselves) and also the harpsichord
player, who unlike most looks truly distressed, tears
pouring down her cheeks, her eyes red (to match her
suit, as elegant as María's but in a very different style
and fabric – a kind of brocade – much less appropriate
than María's for a funeral, but certainly very elegant,
though she's finding it hard to walk on the cobbles,
her heels are too high), then there are the orchestra
musicians (another black cat crosses the path, the
ladies cross themselves again) from the orchestra Juan
conducted, all of them, all the men at least, taking turns
to carry the dead man, passing the coffin among them,
the box wobbling on the shoulders of the pallbearers as
they walk along the path, stumbling on loose stones or
slipping on the cows' excrement and crying: shit!, but
very quietly, it would have to be quietly, seeing as they're
at a funeral, or else the imprecation would be out of

keeping with the perfectly cut, navy blue blazer they bought in London or New York, wouldn't it? The thin, blonde woman, too, the one who is the companion or partner of the tall brunette, has got cow dung all over her shoes and says the word: shit!, quietly but audibly, just like the man in the dark grey and white pinstriped Chicago gangster suit, both of them slipped in cow dung, one after another, as they marched along the rocky path accompanying the dead man, perhaps it was even the same shit, the same cowshit, in the same spot where they both, the drunk man and the thin, well-dressed woman, the one accompanying the taller blonde woman, those two women wearing white, all of them, the drunk man and the woman and the other woman, the one with the clouded pupil, at different moments but in quick succession, stepped and got covered in shit, her designer shoes, the beggar's broken huaraches, his left foot stained with blood, and the shiny black Church's belonging to the official wearing a navy blue, gold-buttoned blazer, they're all covered in dust: he's about to slip, he's just stepped in the very same cowpat and uttered that same word: shit!

They arrive, we arrive at the convent, the cortège slowly enters the church, the coffin is set down near the main altar, the men and their shoulders relax, the funeral mass begins, the priest starts his sermon, a litany recited in a mediocre voice, flat despite being shrill, and when he falls silent the mariachis sing with their limited range, unable to reach the high notes, notes of revenge, fury, machismo, like third-rate Pedro Infantes, and their gestures express their bitterness, only slightly muted or exaggerated by the alcohol they've drunk. The leafless wreaths speak of a municipal salary, near the church there's a lorry trailer packed with motorbikes, the traffic cops a bit further down the road, bribable and bandy-legged in their faded, poorly cut, coffee-coloured suits (black or café-au-lait). In the four corners of the square are stands selling carnitas, quesadillas, chorizo, Delicados cigarettes, pastries, sandwiches, Gansitos, and the mourners, some entering the church, others milling around the entrance, others eating tacos in the square, while in the church mass is being sung, a melancholy mass led by the priest's tuneless voice and the mariachis. Juan is in his coffin surrounded by altar candles and covered in flowers, a stiff body with a sallow face and sallow clothes, a cross clutched against his chest (she wore a blue beret, and a cross hung round her neck), a shabby, straw-coloured moustache over a toothless mouth held firmly in place by a black handkerchief supporting his jaw. And this whole time, like a litany, a rosary, a prayer, indifferent to the people singing, praying, responding to the priest's words, indifferent to those staggering around outside, bragging, accompanying the mariachis' incessant singing, the smell is still dogging me, a persistent, cloying smell, a heavy smell of damp. A man passes me − is he a notary, the one who'll inventory the dead man's belongings? − the pianos (how strange, I say to myself, I only saw the Bösendorfer, the Steinway has disappeared! Could Juan have sold it? Schubert can only be played on a Bösendorfer), the violins, books, sheet music, CDs, paintings, armchairs, portraits, the ordinary pine wood chair where I sat, near the coffin, opposite María; the crockery, sheets, towels, casserole dishes, frying pans, the four bottles of Zhdanov disinfectant. The things, in short, all the things, it's always things, the things that survive the dead. In the church, the beggar, who smells like alcohol, sits on a nearby pew, a freshly bloodied, dirty, shit-smeared bandage on one of his huarache-clod feet, and he too is praying. Sobs can be heard, interrupting the priest's words, the mariachis' singing, and the persistent muttering of a handful of mourners, and people look around curiously: it's a young, dark-skinned man, beardless and not very tall, crying openly, his mother consoling him, he continues to cry and the beggar looks on in astonishment: aren't men not supposed to cry? And I observe him, too, turning round (are we supposed to offer him our condolences?) (is he the only one genuinely affected by this death?) (am I?) (someone ought to offer me their condolences, I think, I feel like I need it, like it's what I really need). I stare impertinently at him until his mother's gaze puts me in my place. I bow my head, wrap myself once again in the smell, the smell that's dogging me, that's followed me from the house to the church, from which the young man's crying gave me a moment of respite. Around me, praying, are other beggars, several black-clad bureaucrats in sweat-stained polyester shirts, women, children, campesinos; the heat intensifies and all their smells fuse with the smell of incense so that the cloying smell disappears for a few moments, lost among the other smells; some people have thick altar candles in their hands; beside the bureaucrat is a woman wearing black glasses and ankle boots, part of their pew is empty and a couple of scraggly-haired men, fresh from the cantina, sit down; there's a heavyset man in shirtsleeves with a provocative gaze, I recognise him, he said hello to me in the house while he was giving orders to the people running around industriously hanging lightbulbs in the trees while the kitchen staff cooked in a makeshift shed using huge aluminium pans over hot coals, women there specially to cook for and attend to the men, the pianists, the fertiliser salesmen, the public transport inspectors, the officials wearing navy blue blazers, the elegant women, the small-town notaries, the self-righteous mourners who've been up all night, the journalists, a cellist, the pianist and the municipal president.

Eduardo is so enormous that to say he is fatuous would be stating the obvious, and yet he is fatuous. He has placed himself next to the tomb, in everyone else's way, his long white beard waving in the wind, taking up almost the entire right-hand side of the grave; he straightens majestically, then looks at me again, I'm opposite him, not particularly close, there's hardly anyone around me, the mourners have followed the cortège into the cemetery's little chapel, he waves at me briefly, his hands swollen from age and excess weight, and I think I see his eyes smile mockingly (what is he laughing at? the sight of me here, opposite him, shrunken?). The party has returned to the church, twice the body has taken its place by the altar, twice the body has been present, once during the mass in the main church then again in the chapel in the cemetery, impassioned and patriotic speeches have been made: the priest, a municipal president, a fertiliser salesman and a singer – the elegant, moustachioed singer who sang a José Alfredo Jiménez song along with the mariachis as though it were an opera aria, and who modulates his voice as though it were a trumpet playing the Dies Irae, without ever quite achieving the solemnity of Mozart's Requiem, nor of Juan's voice as he told us of the death of Bishop Fernández de Santa Cruz – they have all fallen silent. People start arriving, a horde of women insist on taking their places right next to the tomb, four men bring the body, which the priest blesses, and then the gravediggers relieve them to begin gradually lowering it into the grave, deep underground, where the clay rebels, the mariachis sing in their raspy voices: I say to you, crying with rage; the women and children sob and throw flowers, camellias, carnations, Madonna lilies, true lilies (the smell of lilies briefly blots out the persistent smell of damp) (I'm off on the train of forgetting) (I'm reminded again of Pergolesi) (the flowers or the red roses) (I'm not coming back, I say to you, crying with rage, I've only a one-way ticket) (the damp smell intensifies). Eduardo is still guarding the tomb – since when was he such good friends with Juan? or has he just decided to pretend he was his best friend? why wasn't he at the church? could he be atheist? an atheist among the incense and crucifixes? why didn't he give the main eulogy then? I lower my head, but a penetrating gaze makes me look up again, it's Eduardo spying on me, does he have a perverse interest in knowing my reactions? His gaze is like that squirrel that resembles a rat.

People badmouth each other at funerals, they gossip, and then when the person they've been talking about shows up they rearrange their faces: what faces are they wearing? how are their faces arranged when I walk past and see them, when I hear threads of conversation (if you want to avoid a heart attack you ought to take aspirin every morning, or even better, twenty drops of garlic over the course of ten days, diluted in tequila)? Conversations I interrupt and in which I sometimes hear my name (are they speaking ill of me?) and as soon as they see me they arrange their faces and pretend, changing the subject (…I'm telling you, this is what I've been saying, they didn't get on well at all, not at all) (it was all for show) (so he said to her: why don't you go to the beach for a couple of days with the kids?) (when she got back the house was empty, completely empty, he'd even taken the carpets) (that's crazy! he was crazy! crazy, sure, but he knew what he was doing, he hadn't completely lost it) (his arteries were clogged) (he had barely any blood left, they did three transfusions: he almost died three times) (a heart attack is as painful as childbirth) (to whom should we offer our condolences?) (there are certain herbs that can help lower cholesterol: Mexican thistle, or a Moctezuma cypress concentrate). While they tell their endless, banal

117

stories, María is eating her own mouth; I'm taken aback by the cloudy eye of the woman in red; I stare in fascination at the beggar's dusty huaraches and bandaged left foot with its still-fresh drops of blood; Juan continues to lie in his coffin with that face that says nothing any more, he's no longer with us, he's in the unfinished white pine wood box with metal fittings, his toothless mouth silent, especially now they've strapped up his chin with a black handkerchief.

I pretend, putting on my poker face as if I haven't heard a thing, making as if I know no one. In truth many faces no longer mean anything to me, I've forgotten them: Eduardo, on the other hand, is impossible to forget, I hear him bragging, surrounded by people, making grandiose gestures with his hands, his giant, aged hands, his grey beard trembling, there's only one woman in the group, the small, slender woman wearing not a shred of makeup, who is listening as though bewitched. Eduardo pauses, the woman seizes her moment and says loudly: only children and drunks tell the truth, and sometimes not even drunks (such a diminutive body, where did that contralto's – castrato's? – voice come from?) (from the bottom of her heart?). She looks at me out of the corner of her eye, she wants to see my reaction, she purses her lips and her face shudders into one giant wrinkle. I continue on my way, ignoring her, heading from group to group without paying too much attention to what they're saying, though some conversations do stick despite their insignificance, or perhaps because of it, because they're insignificant and they distract me: no, repeats a short, very dark-skinned man with rosy cheeks, very thick glasses and a pipe in his hand, displaying one wrinkled nail, swollen and deformed, I'm telling you, he says, Joaquín's going to win, I can feel it in my bones.

I bow my head, feeling sick, words chase me, the smell envelops me, it's been hounding me since the living room where we held the vigil, it floated all the way into the street and from the street it rose up to the church, although the young man's tears (heartfelt tears, bursting with genuine pain) allowed me a brief respite. Several people are praying near me. The cloying smell comes back and then disappears for a few moments, swallowed by the smell of the altar candles, the thick altar candles some mourners are carrying, and by the young dark-skinned man's tears; a woman dressed in dark grey, wearing glasses and flat, very sober, elegant shoes, has come over and sat down on the same pew as me, it's María. The beggar has disappeared and several scraggly-haired men are making themselves comfortable on the pew behind me, having come straight from the cantina. I suddenly feel a sting, or rather an itch (something is biting me, my whole body is itching, how embarrassing!), how strange, I think, and also how ridiculous: scratching oneself at a funeral: the itch only gets worse, however, and I scratch myself furtively (it feels delicious). I mustn't forget I'm in church, this is a solemn occasion, I'm listening to a funeral mass, there are a lot of people here: I start to come out in a rash, like I've been lying naked in a red ants' nest, my whole body is itching, maybe I've got scabies? or is it some effect of that damp smell? some wild allergy to the people around me? or is this some sophisticated somatisation of grief? Will they offer me their condolences now?

The party is about to head back, the body has twice lain by the altar, twice been present, once in the mass in the main church then again in the cemetery chapel, he's been sent off with impassioned and patriotic speeches, spoken from the heart: the priest, a municipal president, a fertiliser salesman and a singer who modulates his voice like a trumpet playing the Dies Irae, although it doesn't quite achieve the solemn percussion of Mozart's Requiem. People are milling around, a horde of women insist on taking their places at the graveside, but Eduardo is stubborn and powerful and stands his ground, prefiguring the monument which, a year later, will immortalise a figure, Juan's figure, in the form of a statue. Four men carry his body, which the priest blesses, then the gravediggers relieve them and gradually lower the coffin into the grave; the women and children sob, throw flowers, camellias, carnations, Madonna lilies, true lilies, Peruvian lilies, stars of Bethlehem, gladioli, camellias (the smell of tuberoses briefly blots out the persistent smell of damp) and finally a red rose, identical to the one Pergolesi's anonymous admirer tosses onto the stage in the Teatro La Argentina in Rome, just as the great composer is crying over his failure, shortly before dying with his heart in pieces.

In the church, while the funeral mass is in progress, I'm reminded of a French film from the end of the 1940s called Le sang des bêtes, in which several enormous men appear, desensitised or impervious to the death and the blood and the stink, and administer a single blow to a white horse, using an instrument that makes a dry thwack and kills instantly, before sinking a sharp knife into the beast's belly or throat, from which black blood gushes: it smokes and burns, they remove its steaming heart, the heart is only a muscle. (A man, egged on by his lover, murders a pregnant woman by stabbing her seven times in the heart, two or three drops of blood drip from her chest (Nastasya Filippovna?), then he takes her eldest son (eight years old) and her six-year-old daughter, slits their throats one after the other with a kitchen knife and throws the bodies into the river: blood gushes.) Repetitive, systematic, ritual movements give it meaning, framing what I'm seeing, fascinated, feeling slightly sick, sitting in front of the television in my house, or in the living room watching the body, listening to María, or in the church while the mass is being given, surrounded by notaries, musicians, officials, women, old men, children and beggars, or by the graveside, standing with Eduardo. It's a greyish, grainy, documentary, the copy is very old, but the blood can be seen clearly, it's thick and black and clots slowly on the version I'm watching; an old version, stained, its colour like that of the suits worn by the charros who, at this wake I arrived at not so long ago and where I'm currently standing near the coffin, are singing outside in their tuneless voices, and all the mourners have a glass of tequila in their hand, talking and smiling. The charros' suits are as faded and dirty as the ones in the documentary, and yet in the documentary you can see the blood falling from the mutilated horse, pooling thickly, spreading, throbbing, lengthening, clotting within seconds; the horse and the men who have wounded him tremble, the blood spills, running over the floor of the old Parisian abattoir where, at the exact moment at which I'm watching, they kill the beast, burying the knife in its throat or stomach or piercing its heart (they remove it, still warm, open-heart surgery is a kind of butchery), then, once the horse is dead, they start to dismember it, to slit its throat, using axes, hammers, saws, they cut through – are cutting through – the bones, they separate – are separating – the fat from the entrails, they focus on the heart, it's smoking, smoking, it's still beating (a hundred beats per minute!) and the body is gradually butchered until only pieces of the beautiful white horse remain, pieces of flesh and bone.

No one has explored the weave of marks or done a combinatorial analysis of the symbolic elements in the image, their function within various homogeneous series established in relation to their origin, to the nature of the objects, the themes depicted there. I couldn't say what role certain animals (snakes, lizards, squirrels, birds, wild creatures, rats, cats, insects, cows, even roses) and, in particular, horses play in the imaginary surrounding the figure of the Gorgon. In figurative depictions, the horse – or horses, arranged symmetrically – appear to be inextricably linked, in image and purpose, to the Gorgon; horses are an extension or emanation of her, like Perseus's horse, Pegasus, who appears as soon as Perseus slices off the Gorgon Medusa's head. In those cases, in which the horse is associated with the Gorgon, an excess or overflow of meaning is produced.

One of the most interesting museums in Boston is the one named after Isabella Stewart Gardner, a millionaire immortalised by John Singer Sargent, a painter Mark Rothko hated because he only painted influential people. In the painting, the woman is wearing a sombre, black, silk dress with a modest neckline that barely suggests the curve of her extremely white chest. The outfit is belted (she is wearing a corset) with two strings of pearls, identical in size and appearance to the ones on the choker around her neck, very fine pearls rounded off by a ruby pendant set in gold. The overskirt exaggerates her hips and makes for a silhouette totally different to today's skeletal models. Her hands are linked together, resting on her stomach in order to accentuate her waist. Ms Gardner isn't wearing make-up, for at the time it would have been a flagrant sign of vulgarity (I remember a famous passage from Proust's novel in which a young woman from the haute bourgeoisie appears lightly made up on a street in Paris: the narrator's grand-mother refuses to speak to her ever again). Behind her, like a halo, a golden silk brocade covers the wall and as you move down the painting she is slowly cast into shadow until the black of the dress melts completely into the background, leaving us to imagine her satin shoes decorated with a ruby brooch.

The Gardner Museum houses furniture, tapestries, paintings, many of them acquired on the advice of Bernard Berenson, a great scholar of Italian painting, one of the first to pay attention to the masters of the first Renaissance revival. Indeed, it's there that you can admire two Mantegnas and several portraits by Uccello and Pollaiuolo depicting young patrician women, a Piero della Francesca portraying Hercules, a painting by Cosimo (or Cosmè Tura, who painted for the d'Este Dukes of Ferrara) and another by the Venetian Carlo Crivelli, which also has Oriental touches – the same painters who line the rooms dedicated to the Italian Quattrocento in the National Gallery in London, and who are mentioned in a beautiful story by the US writer Edith Wharton: she tells the story of a young heir from New England whose taste shows a delicate, morbid interest, avant la lettre, a pale aesthete who, on his obligatory trip through Italy, acquires paintings with no market value (the same ones we can admire in the Isabella Stewart Gardner Museum), for which lapse in judgement his father disinherits him.

The museum is an old Venetian palace relocated from Italy to New England, where objects in dreadful taste coexist with masterpieces – curtains, Japanese folding screens, furniture, stained glass windows, sublime paintings, like for example one by Sofonisba Anguissola, the Italian painter who lived in the court of Philip II and painted like Claudio Coello. The house is built around a loggia where there's a winter garden with orchids and several lemon trees producing a kind of giant, lustrous yellow grapefruit, where the green of the leaves on the bush is only comparable to trees painted in the Renaissance, and from the windows of the bedroom where the Virgin receives the angel Gabriel you can see a landscape as unreal as the green of the leaves and the blue of the sky. Alongside the lemon trees are wild (ferocious) orchids, giant ferns and mutilated statues.

I saw a small exhibition there dedicated to Cosimo Tura, bringing together about twelve small paintings – it's a very special exhibition, says the museum guard in response to a visitor who asks, disappointed, why there are so few pieces on display. Two paintings stand out: one small one of a Virgin Mary dressed in cherry-coloured velvet (very like the colour of the Emmanuelle Khanh suit María is wearing), very simple, although a little low-cut, and in her lap lies the son of God with an adult face, half-smiling, reflective. On the wall opposite, the most important painting in the small exhibition is a Pietà showing the desolate Mary sitting on a tomb (an exquisitely carved stone sarcophagus) with Christ's body still convulsing in her lap, displaying the suffering of a martyr, his lips an intense purple colour, parted to allow us a glimpse of his very white teeth which contrast with his livid, or even purplish skin, the same tone as the mother's mantle, the stiff, heavy, sculptural folds of which fall to the ground, framing the body of Christ. The Virgin is wearing a black dress that shows off part of her neck, while her head (in three-quarter profile) is covered with a piece of gauze that completely hides her hair: she lifts her son's right arm to her face as though to kiss it (wearing an expression of profound sadness). She is the same age as Christ, who, naked, his lower abdomen covered by a gauze similar to her head covering, holds his left hand over his belly so the puncture wound from the nail is visible, and drops of bright red, freshly-spilled blood draw attention to the wound in his side, too: his face looks Asian, its grotesque agony exaggerated by the slender crown of thorns from which two clear trickles of blood are running. Behind them, a strange landscape,

Golgotha, a mountain in the shape of a spiral which, like the Tower of Babel, rises, twisting, with three crosses atop it, two bearing the writhing bodies of the thieves, the central one unoccupied.

Tura's figures, says Berenson, look like they were carved from stone, as hieratic and immobile as statues of Egyptian pharaohs, but their fitful, contained energy is like the knots interrupting a slender olive trunk. Tura differs from his contemporaries, from the Florentine Sandro Botticelli, for example, whose idea of beauty is one of delicate and classical simplicity.

I keep watching the documentary almost a week after the funeral – one of the butchers is cruel and fat, with a dark face from another era (the squirrel is watching me from the window, its eyes have softened, they're no longer like rats' eyes). Suddenly, his axe slips, and instead of delivering another blow to the horse's body the butcher catches his own leg and blood flows again, steaming, black, and everything ends, the screen goes dark and then a moment, just a moment later, so quick you barely catch it, the camera shows the man again but with one healthy leg and one prosthetic one – he's not a butcher any more, I say to myself, he's a pirate – the left leg, the one he cut off with the axe, is now a stump resting on an old fashioned prosthesis; the axe, the same axe, is still moving masterfully, still butchering, still murdering horses in the abattoir, that old French abattoir in a Parisian suburb, a pre-Second World War Paris that's dark and humble, a Paris that looks like the Paris in Brassaï's photographs, and this documentary I'm watching right now, or which I'm remembering now, next to the coffin, looking at him, at Juan, listening to María and watching her vanishing mouth, her mutilated face, her lips pressed bitterly together, I remember the horses' butchered bodies piling up, more and more, the bodies of more mutilated horses, the stink unbearable now, I can feel the horror and nausea through the screen. I'm still looking at the wasted body in front of me, plagued by that cloying smell that surrounds me like a halo, it won't leave me, it won't leave him, and in that precise moment several strong, brutish men appear on the screen, head for the enormous room where the mutilated butcher is wielding his axe, and gradually, one by one, arrange the pieces of the chopped-up beasts on wide, wheeled platforms so they can load the trucks that will deliver the horse meat to the meat traders who stock it: life is an absurd wound. Horse meat doesn't taste the same as beef, it tastes sweet, and its sweetness is repulsive. I still dream that I'm lost: when I wake up I never know where I am, I can't bear it, it makes me furious, my heart racing.

In Georgia, in a crematorium where dead people are supposedly incinerated, corpses have been discovered in different stages of decomposition. The relatives had received urns full of nothing but earth and lime.

I'm by the coffin, I can feel the blood flowing around my body, I can feel my guts twisting, his guts, and with my heart already aching from misfortune I remember the blood spilling into the horse's eyes or running down the butcher's leg when, surprised by the blow, he looks down at the axe in his hand, the axe which has slipped and accidentally – accidentally? – mutilated him, as though he, he too, were a horse. I feel my blood again, nothing but blood, then bile, nothing but bile, dry bitterness, suppressed rage, hate turning on me as though I were infected and my violence were a contagion spreading, attacking, threatening to burst through my skin, to let the blood pour out, blood the butcher has made gush from his severed leg, the blood that runs down to the floor to accompany the leg that's falling and the face that sees it, out of orbit, the axe still in his hand, warm, viscous, filthy, his eyes fixed on his own blood, the blood that leaks from a heart when a heart is broken (they've replaced the mitral valve with a valve made from animal tissue) (either from a pig or a cow) or when they open up a chest (open-heart surgery), your broken heart in my hands (the damaged arteries have been replaced with grafts, they've used delicate arteries from mammary glands) (or they've made a bridge using the saphenous vein), the blood mingled with the horse's blood spilt on the stained floor of the slaughterhouse and a cloying smell emanating from the screen, identical to this cloying smell that's been following me and which not even the smell of flowers (mainly tuberoses), not even roses can lessen, not even red roses, just as the four unstoppered bottles of (Zhdanov) disinfectant couldn't manage to blot out the persistent rotting smell given off by Nastasya Filippovna's decomposing body (Rogozhin had thought of surrounding Nastasya's body with roses but he doesn't, he's horrified by the idea that anyone could (even) imagine she might be dead). That cloying smell won't fade, not even with the scent of the flowers, not with the smell nor the swell of the altar candles: four, that's right, arranged at the four corners of the coffin.

I'm alone, sitting in front of the screen, hypnotised, watching the documentary over and over, smelling the spilled blood despite in reality there being no blood in this sallow body over which we are holding vigil. This body has been drained.

Drained? I wonder. The word, said aloud like that, or murmured, makes me think immediately of a body in which blood has ceased to flow: a body that no longer actually contains any blood. Life is an absurd wound: I think I deserve to be offered condolences. It's obvious, in a live body blood circulates constantly (the heart tissue weighs two hundred and fifty to three hundred grams and has a rhythm of fifty to a hundred beats per minute, or a hundred thousand times a day) (Glenn Gould made his final recording of the Goldberg Variations in fifty-one minutes, fifteen seconds, in 1981) and this body, Juan's body, is no longer living, it is dead, his heart has not a single beat left in it, which simply means – I repeat this quietly, ad infinitum, without really understanding – it simply means that the blood no longer flows, it no longer runs through his veins, his heart has stopped beating (fifty or a hundred beats per minute), the blood, I repeat, blood, blood cannot flow when a body dies and when the muscle known as the heart has necrotised.

The heart has motives that reason does not know, Pascal said.

I dreamed I was lost. I woke up furious: I have not found myself (my blood pressure has gone up).

The body over which I'm holding vigil, in the living room of the huge house where I'm accompanied by a thick, constant smell of altar candles and tuberoses and mildew, is lying in a coffin made of pale, unfinished wood with gold fittings, dressed in an olive green suit and a nondescript tie, holding a cross to his chest, his face livid and dislocated, his eyes sunken, a wispy, faded moustache above his violet, toothless mouth, his jaw bound with a black handkerchief to stop it falling open, his beautiful hands, his long, elegant, sallow fingers. This body, I conclude, no longer has any blood in it.

It is a drained, bloodless body.

A dead body

Coyoacán, Princeton, Coyoacán,
Harvard, Coyoacán,
1999, 2001–2002

c

TRANSLATOR'S NOTE

On Variation

Written as a long monologue, *The Remains* follows Nora
García as she attends the funeral of her ex-husband, Juan,
who has recently died of a heart attack. Without ever
quite leaving the present tense, we shift temporally from
the funeral, held in the house where she once lived, to
scenes from her life with him, to a future moment in
which she is writing an account of the funeral, and back
again, various times. As we make these shifts, a picture
slowly emerges of Juan as, at best, the quintessential
mansplainer, and of Nora unable to quite decide how
she feels about his death.

But this rich novel-cum-essay is much more than a
basic plot outline can suggest. More than anything, it is
a unique experiment in form: a set of literary variations.
In music, variation is a basic composition technique
in which the same musical material is repeated in an
altered form. A single piece of music might include
multiple sections based on the same melody but played
each time at a different tempo, or in counterpoint
with another melody, or with a different timbre or

orchestration. Variations were especially popular in the baroque era, and Bach's *Goldberg Variations* – discussed at length in the novel – with its thirty variations on a single lengthy theme, is a monument to this compositional style. In fiction, however, repetition and variation is not something we come across often, or certainly not on the scale witnessed here.

Nora digresses often, returning obsessively to the same fragments of songs, poems, and other literary texts, though each time in a slightly different guise. Readers of English may be familiar with some of her cultural reference points, such as Dostoyevsky's *The Idiot*, but not necessarily all of them: snippets from the 1943 tango 'Tristeza marina' or the Mexican ranchera 'No volveré', or lines from the Maya miscellanies known as the Books of Chilam Balam are perhaps less likely to be recognised. Some of the most important source texts are included here as epigraphs: a seventeenth-century sonnet by Sor Juana Inés de la Cruz in which a lover's heart is distilled into tears, and a 1956 tango titled 'La última curda' ('One Final Binge'), with lyrics by Cátulo Castillo and music by Aníbal Troilo. She also returns over and over again to the idea of the heart, dissecting it, examining it from the perspectives of art, literature, music, film, and the history of science, making this novel, like much of Glantz's work, unapologetically erudite.

The technique of repetition and variation means *The Remains* is expansive, loose, rich in adjectives. It contains few sentences and even fewer paragraphs. In general, Spanish prose is more accommodating than English of run-on sentences and comma splices, but this novel positively revels in them. Translating it, I had to remind myself that, despite a preference for extreme concision and precision in the classrooms of contemporary anglophone creative writing courses, the English language can handle being stretched and folded and stretched again. It is versatile and resilient. Think of the success of Lucy Ellmann's *Ducks, Newburyport*, I told myself, over a thousand pages long but with just eight sentences and innumerable clauses all beginning with 'the fact that'. Think of the popularity of Fernanda Melchor's *Hurricane Season* in Sophie Hughes's translation, another contemporary Mexican classic whose paragraph-less prose roars through its pages, leaving readers reeling. In *The Remains*, too, it was imperative not to diminish the novel's breathless, relentless rhythm – its beating heart, the metronome's pulse.

Strangely enough, translating Glantz's apparently loose, iterative style demanded unusual precision, because every slight variation in her expression of an idea or image contributes to the structural coherence of the whole. It helps depict a protagonist on the verge of collapse – a woman who focuses obsessively on details to postpone having to confront a mixture of grief, rage, and resentment. It matters that Nora at first perceives Juan's jacket to be the colour of hay, and then burnt straw, and then moss, and then olive. It matters that she contradicts herself. It matters that she gets song lyrics slightly wrong. Over the course of the novel, Glantz writes (I write):

The heart has reasons that reason does not know.
The heart has impulses that reason does not know.
The heart has reasons that intelligence does not know.
The heart has secret designs that reason does not know.
The heart has motives that reason does not know.

These variations on Blaise Pascal's famous dictum 'Le coeur a ses raisons que la raison ne connaît point' are themselves a lesson in translation: in its fluidity, its impermanence, its perpetual malleability. Paper and ink give the false impression of fixity but the work of a translator involves constant movement, a repeated pivoting between infinitesimally different versions. I could translate this book over and over again until the end of time and still not be convinced it was finished. But then again, neither is the novel – the final words on the final page of *The Remains* are not followed by a full stop. Nora García's consciousness streams on. And on, in this new variation in English.

Ellen Jones
Mexico City, August 2022

CHARCO PRESS

Director & Editor: Carolina Orloff
Director: Samuel McDowell

www.charcopress.com

The Remains was published on
90gsm Munken Premium Cream paper.

The text was designed using Bembo 11.5 and ITC Galliard.

Printed in January 2023 by TJ Books
Padstow, Cornwall, PL28 8RW using responsibly
sourced paper and environmentally-friendly adhesive.